Love's Early Hours

Love's Early Hours

Nathan Jay

JNJ Publishing LLC

CONTENTS

1 | Decisions　1

2 | Advice and Goodbyes　5

3 | No Turning Back　11

4 | Guilt　14

5 | The Arrival　17

6 | Checking in With Mom　24

7 | The Return to Crazy　30

8 | House Cleaning　33

9 | Night Life　37

10 | Everyone Knows　43

11 | Calling it a Night　46

12 | Disgusting Things at The Ungodly Hour　51

13 | The Truth Always Comes Out　55

CONTENTS

14 | The New Repeat 60

15 | Determined 65

16 | Onward 69

17 | Closer to the Dream 73

18 | Six Months Later 80

19 | What a Day 83

20 | Seeking Comfort Through Pain 90

21 | Told You So 93

22 | Misery 96

23 | You Cannot Run Forever 98

24 | A Night Without Men 102

25 | What Love is Worth 109

26 | Motherly Advice 111

27 | One Month Later 116

28 | The Clarity of Being Single (2 Months Later) 120

29 | Another Six Months Behind You 127

30 | Next Level 131

31 | Lightning in the Clouds 135

32 | Descent 138

33 | Criminals 144

34 | Sign of Power 149

35 | 2 Months Later 152

36 | Back Home 155

37 | Recall 158

38 | The Slow Life 161

39 | Rough Roads Revisited 163

40 | Breaking the News 168

41 | The Truth About the World 171

Decisions

Janice sat on the playground, watching her little brother climbing on the monkey bars.

"Hey, Janice! Look at what I can do!" the little boy yelled.

After positioning his legs between the bars, he flipped his body upside down.

"Wow, Trevor. That's awesome!" Janice replied.

Her little brother was growing up, and soon he would be in the third grade. As she stared at the sun setting in the distance, a feeling of sadness came over her. Her whole world was about to change, and the people she'd been with for years would soon be gone. Suddenly her brother let go of the monkey bars and landed on his feet.

"Trevor, you need to be careful doing tricks like that. You could get hurt."

"Oh, that's nothing. I can do flips better than a superhero."

Janice giggled at the child's courage.

"I'll bet you could."

Trevor was about to climb on the bars to demonstrate his underestimated skill once again when he saw something in the distance.

"Nick!" Trevor yelled as he sprinted in the direction of the approaching shadow. Janice turned towards the street and saw her boyfriend Nick, walking towards her. Instead of greeting him, she turned back to face the jungle gym.

"Hi, Trevor! How's it going?" replied Nick.

As he approached, the child became anxious to show off.

"Hey, Nick. Do you want to see the neat trick I learned?"

"Sure, little guy. Show me."

As soon as Trevor took off running towards the monkey bars, Nick went to sit on the bench closest to Janice.

"You know if my step-dad sees us together, he's going to kill you."

"I know, but I can't stay away."

"It seems like forever since I last saw you."

"It's been one month and three days."

Janice smiled. It felt nice to know that Nick missed her just as much as she missed him.

"I just wish..."

"What? That we didn't get caught?"

"Yeah, me too. But it was worth it."

Janice wasn't so sure. She remembered the anger in her stepdad's eyes when he opened the door to her bedroom and saw Nick's naked butt climbing out the window. It was a look that terrified her. She was sure that if her stepdad had his gun when he walked into the room, her boyfriend would be dead.

"My stepdad isn't playing, Nick. He said he'd shoot you if you come anywhere near me again."

"And you believe him?"

"All of those animal heads aren't hanging in our house because he's gun shy."

"Well, it won't matter in a few hours."

Janice inched her hand close to his and took his pinky finger in hers.

"I missed you," she whispered.

Her whole body trembled at the touch of Nick's warm hand.

"I missed you too," he replied. "You ready?"

"As ready as I'll ever be, I suppose."

"You packed?"

"I'll do that tonight after everyone goes to sleep. What about you?"

"I'm packed. My bag is under my bed with all the other stuff."

"Remind me, how much money do you have saved?"

"$2000. And you?"

"A little over five grand."

"Did you tell your mom you're going away?"

"Are you crazy? She would run straight to my stepdad, and he'd be at your house ready to shoot you."

There was silence as the two lovers watched the little boy hanging upside down.

"Are you sure you want to go through with this, Nick?"

"Why? Aren't you? Are you afraid of what your stepdad will do?"

"Not if we leave. Michael's not even my real dad anyway. He's just pretending to give a damn. I'm sure he wants me gone just as much as I want to be gone. It's just that…"

"What?"

"I won't see Trevor for a long time. It's not his fault his father's a jerk. We might be half-siblings, but he's my brother. We look out for one another. If I leave, who will look out for him?"

"It's something we can't avoid. You just said your stepdad is crazy. Michael's not going to let us be together."

"Yeah, but to leave so abruptly. A lot of feelings are going to get hurt."

"Look, Janice. We've already talked about this. We can take control of our lives and make a move, or we can stay here. I can't live without you. Do you want to let your stepfather break us up? Is that what you want?"

"You know it's not. I can't live without you, Nick. Now that we've found each other, I can't go back to being alone."

"Then what choice do we have? God forbid your stepdad finds out I'm 21. I'm toast if that happens."

Janice agreed. She was only 17, and Michael would flip out if he knew her boyfriend's real age. Not to mention the fact that her mother would lose it.

"Promise me you won't ever leave me."

Nick looked deep into her eyes.

"I promise you that I will love you forever. I will never leave you. I swear to God."

Unable to control her emotions, Janice leaned over and kissed Nick.

"I will never leave you either. I'm yours forever, Nick."

Janice shot a glance at her brother as he hung upside down. As soon as Trevor wasn't looking, she stole another kiss from her boyfriend.

"Okay, let's do it."

"Good. I'll see you at midnight."

Suddenly Janice's little brother's hands slipped from the metal bars, and he fell face first in the sawdust. Janice jumped up and ran to the child.

"Trevor! Are you okay?"

The boy stood and brushed the pieces of wood from his face.

"I'm okay. Superheroes don't get hurt."

After brushing the remaining dust from her brother's clothes, Janice turned to continue talking to Nick.

"Hey, maybe we should…"

But Nick was gone.

Advice and Goodbyes

"What do you have planned with your friends this weekend?"

Janice was a little surprised by her mother's question, and she almost dropped the plate she was drying.

"What?"

"You and Christy. I heard you talking on the phone about taking a trip. What do you guys have planned?"

Janice quickly looked away. She'd been talking on the phone with Nick about their plans. If her mom had listened a little while longer, she would've discovered who was on the other end of the phone.

"Planned?"

"Come on. What is it, something for your birthday next month?"

"Oh, yeah. Christy was talking about going to the carnival. It's supposed to come in a week or two."

Janice's mother nudged her with her elbow as she grabbed another plate from the dish rack.

"Are you girls going alone or with a bunch of guys?"

"Mom, come on."

"It's okay. You can tell me. I remember when your father took me to the carnival when we were dating. We had so much fun. I still think about it to this day."

"He's not my father, mom."

"He may as well be. He's been with you your whole life."

Janice exhaled in frustration. Her mom was always trying to bridge the gap between reality and fantasy -fantasy being that Michael loved Janice as his own and fact being that Janice would never accept Michael as her father. Janice tried to change the subject.

"It's just a girl trip, mom."

"You sure you aren't planning a trip somewhere else? I heard you talking about bus fares. Carnivals don't require bus fares."

"What do you think we're going to Europe or something?"

"You kids nowadays aren't into simple things like carnivals. Today all the kids are into traveling to exotic places they've never been and doing risky things. I'll tell you what, sometimes simple is better. When we were young, I had the most romantic dates at those carnivals."

Janice put away the plate in the cabinet and turned to face her mom.

"If you had your life to do over, would you do everything the same way?"

"What do you mean?"

"I mean, didn't you have dreams? What if you could've done anything else? Would you have still chosen the same life?"

"This is about that boy your father caught you with, isn't it?"

"Michael's my stepdad, mom. And no, it isn't about that."

"Well, you know we didn't raise you like that. I'm with Michael on this one. You had no right to disrespect our home like that. That boy's lucky we didn't call the cops."

Janice was becoming angry.

"It's not about Nick, mom. Can't we talk like a regular mother and daughter without you judging me?"

Janice's mother peered around the corner into the other room. After making sure no one was coming, she spoke.

"You want to know a secret?"

"What?"

"Michael and I got caught doing it in the car on Silver's Lake."
Janice's mouth dropped open.
"Mom!"

"Yeah. We had been married for only one year, and we were out at the lake on a date night. The cops caught us."

"So, how can you judge me if you did the same thing?"

"For one, we were married. Two, we didn't disrespect our family by having sex in their house. And three, we were in our thirties."

Janice looked at her mom and became nauseous. She couldn't imagine her mom and her stepdad doing something so disgusting.

"That's just between you and me," whispered her mother.

At that moment, Janice's stepdad walked into the kitchen. He opened the refrigerator and stuck his head inside.

"What's the big secret?" he asked.

Janice's mother tapped her on the hand and signaled for her to be quiet.

"Oh, nothing. Just mother and daughter talk."

"It had better not be about that son of a bitch I caught in my house."

Janice sighed and looked away while her mother attempted to change the subject.

"Can I watch some tv now? You've been hogging it the whole day."

"Game's on."

Janice's stepfather looked back suspiciously at them and returned to searching the refrigerator.

"This is the last beer. Shannon, did you go shopping today?" Michael asked, interrupting the conversation.

Janice took one look at her stepfather with his pants hanging half off his ass and walked to the other side of the kitchen.

"Michael, you know you get paid on Thursday. Why would I do the shopping now? I'll be sure to pick some up tomorrow."

Michael grabbed the beer and slammed the refrigerator in protest. As he exited the kitchen, he let out a loud wet fart. Shannon cracked a smile and turned to her daughter. Janice was doing her best to wave away from the foul odor.

"Would I do things differently? Possibly, but who's to say? Reality is different than fantasy. Sure, every woman on this planet wants to run for congress, have a tight-butt model for a husband, and gobs of money. But the reality of it is I have a job as a part-time teacher that barely pays above minimum wage, a husband with a beer belly that farts on Wednesday nights, and I'm one month behind on the electric bill."

"So, you wouldn't change anything?"

"Janice, what is this about? Seriously, I'm not dumb, you know. If you're upset about us not wanting you with that boy, there are plenty of other nice boys out there."

"No, mom. It's not about a boy. It's about getting the most out of my life. I don't want to be…"

"What? Poor? Regular? Spit it out, girl."

"I feel like…"

Janice reconsidered what she was about to say. Her mom was like a hound dog when it came to sensing trouble.

"I want to take advantage of all life has to offer."

"Well, you're doing that, right?"

"Mostly. I don't want to make the same mistakes as girls in my high school."

Suddenly a frightened look came across Shannon's face. She moved close to her daughter and lowered her voice.

"Oh, my God. You're pregnant!"

"Jesus, mom. No! It's nothing like that."

"Are you sure? I'm not ready to be a grandmother. Not now."

"It's not that, mom. I promise you. It's just that I don't want to end up like you."

"Like me? What's wrong with my life?"

"Barely making it. Being with a man that hits you."

Shannon lowered her voice.

"Now wait a minute, Janice. You're out of line."

"Oh, come on, mom. Is this how you saw yourself when you were young? I've seen the bruises and the black eyes. You can't tell me that it's okay."

Shannon turned away from her daughter and grabbed the broom.

"What do you want? A way to avoid every problem before you crash into it? It doesn't exist with love. You go in blindly, and you smash into a few things before you find your way."

"I want to be with someone that loves me and would never do those things."

"You think I don't? Everyone does. Things just happen."

"Not for me. I want real love. Good love."

"Unlike your real piece-of-shit dad, Michael knows what responsibility is, and he loves me. Sure, sometimes things go off the rails, but that doesn't mean you run away. Sometimes running isn't the solution."

"Staying and getting beat up isn't either."

"Young people see things so clearly. No fog. Just wait until life sneaks up on you. Wait until you have a child and your closest relative is in another state. Let's see which wars you choose to wage."

"I'll bet my real dad never hit you."

Janice's mother stopped sweeping and stared at her.

"Your real father is gone, Janice. He hasn't spent a single day in his selfish life giving two fucks about you or me. Where is this coming from? Why are you blaming me for his decisions?"

"His decisions?"

"That's right. Your real father left me as soon as he found out I was pregnant."

"I don't believe that."

"You can believe what you want to believe. But Michael didn't hesitate in dating a woman with a kid. He took you in and tried to raise you as his own. And in God's eyes, that's honorable. Meanwhile, who knows where the hell your real dad is and who cares? A man that skates out on his responsibilities always pays the price down the road."

"And overlooking the abuse Michael gives you is an easy price to pay, right?"

"Call it what you want, but I know where Michael's heart is. The question is, do you?"

Janice put up her last dish and kissed her mother on the cheek.

"I don't want to fight, mom. Goodnight."

"Goodnight."

As Janice walked past her stepdad watching tv in the den, she glared at him with hatred in her eyes. He returned her glare with his own and took a sip of beer. Janice knew he heard the whole conversation, but she didn't care. Any man that would beat her mother was a piece of shit in her book.

"Those dishes had better be clean," he mumbled as she passed.

Janice ignored him. She'd made her decision. She was leaving with Nick at midnight.

3

No Turning Back

Janice smiled when she saw Nick sitting at the bus station. He was wearing the conservative clothes they both agreed he should, a plain brown t-shirt and blue jeans with a baseball cap. Janice wore the same bland choice of clothing, except she chose to wear a black hoodie tied around her waist just in case she got cold on the bus ride. As soon as she entered the building, Nick stood up to greet her.

"Got the tickets," Nick said as he took her bag.

Janice smiled and kissed him. She took a step back and looked him over.

"You're looking plain. I never would've picked you out in a crowd."

"That's the point, isn't it? We don't want to look like dumb ass country folks lost in the big city."

They both sat down on a bench and stared at the electronic board for arriving buses. The impact of Janice's decision and what she was about to do finally hit her.

"I can't believe we're doing this," she whispered while clutching Nick's arm. "Are you sure about this?"

Nick looked deep into Janice's eyes.

"I've never been surer about something in my life."

Janice felt butterflies in her stomach. Life was so simple with Nick. Their love was like a train that wouldn't stop, no matter who got in their way. Still, leaving her family was a big decision that she wasn't sure she'd given enough consideration.

"You want to hear something funny?" she asked, trying to suppress the doubt lingering in her mind.

"Sure. Shoot."

"Mom and my stepdad got busted for having sex in public when they first got married."

"Are you serious? Mr. and Mrs. Live By the Bible?"

"Yep. Mom confessed last night. I think she feels a little bad that my stepdad escalated things."

"I'm not surprised. Teenagers fuck. That's just a fact of life. I don't see why Michael had to make such a big deal out of it."

"Well, I am living under his roof. How would you feel if some dude you didn't know was…"

"What? Fucking?"

Janice frowned in disapproval.

"Do you have to speak so vulgar?"

Nick moved close to her and ran his tongue gently on her neck.

"Weren't you yelling that word when I had your legs up and…"

Janice's eyes widened. She pushed her boyfriend away and looked around.

"Nick! Not in public!"

"Okay, okay. You can be just like an old lady sometimes."

"I am not."

"One thing's for sure. You'd better get used to hearing language you don't like. Washington, DC, is filled with politicians, and I'm sure you're going to hear that talk daily."

Janice's eyes began to sparkle when she heard the words Washington, DC.

"I wonder what the city will be like?"

"Different than this little town, I'm sure. Busy, busy, and busier. Everybody is running around like chickens with their heads cut off."

"Maybe we should've chosen New York."

"Are you crazy? Remember Jude? He went to New York and lost all his money in one month. He told me the rent was $3000 for a studio apartment. And that wasn't even counting food and transportation costs."

"Jesus! I hope you found something cheaper for us."

"I told you, I've got it all planned out. In the beginning, we'll be renting a room out of this lady's townhouse. I saw her ad in a DC newspaper online. It's only $600 per month. I figure with the money we've saved, you and I can find jobs before the money runs out."

"Jobs. That sounds so – adult."

"Well, you can't chase your dreams with empty pockets. Besides, I did my research. DC has a lot of opportunities for artists like you. The city has so much culture and tons of inspiration. And it works for me too because I want to join a band."

"I know you didn't tell your mom and dad you wanted to be in a band."

"I wake up the whole neighborhood with my guitar every Saturday. Sure they know. But I guess they didn't know how intense I was about pursuing my dreams."

Suddenly the electronic board lit up with bus arrivals. Nick looked at the two tickets he purchased and compared them to the bus numbers flashing on the screen.

"That's us. Let's go."

Nick grabbed both their bags, and they walked to board their bus.

4

Guilt

"Shit. Some of that nasty blue water splashed on my shoe," complained Nick as he sat down.

Janice moved close to the window and looked down at his feet.

"Well, don't get it on me."

"What? You won't love me if I'm a little smelly?"

Janice pecked Nick on the lips and then reached above her head to turn off the small light shining down on them. She stared out the bus window at the city lights closest to the highway and checked her watch.

"What is it?"

"My mom and stepdad are probably worrying now. In a few minutes, they'll be calling a few of my friends."

"Or the cops."

"*And* the cops."

"Didn't you leave a letter for them?"

"Of course, I did. Whether I left a note or not, my mom and stepdad will freak out when they walk in the house and I'm not there."

"You didn't tell them what city we're going to, did you?"

"No, but mom isn't stupid. Neither is Michael. They'll know you're involved."

"Great. Your stepdad and mom will probably think I kidnapped you or something."

Janice thought a moment.

"Maybe you should call your parents."

"What? That's crazy!"

"How are you going to get a job if you have a warrant for your arrest? Call your parents and explain what we've decided. Tell them to visit my house so that everything gets calmed before things get out of hand. I'll call my mom too."

"But you know this wasn't a part of the plan."

"I know. But we have to at least try to stop our parents from going berserk."

Nick laid his head back on the seat.

"No," he finally whispered.

"No?" asked Janice.

"Part of the reason we're leaving is to start our own lives. What do you think is going to happen if you speak to your mom?"

"Our parents will be relieved?"

"Relieved? That's a joke. As soon as you get on the phone with your mom, she's going to start crying. Next thing you know, you're crying. Two or three days after that, we're climbing on a bus to go back home. What's the point in doing that?"

Janice was about to disagree until she thought about her relationship with her mom. Nick had a point. Her mom knew which buttons to push to get what she wanted. Crying was her most potent weapon.

"So, we're just not going to call them? What about the police?"

"We can call them, but we'll be smart about it. We'll call and leave messages when we know they're at work. If we dial the number and they answer, we'll hang up the phone. It's better if we avoid holding conversations with them until we get settled. After all, it's not like we're kids. I'm 21, and you're almost 18."

"And you're sure this is the best way?"

"I'm positive."

"Okay, we'll do it your way. But whatever problems come with the police, you're going to need to own up to it."

Nick placed his head on Janice's shoulder and closed his eyes.

"We're making the right decision. You'll see."

Janice turned and continued staring out the window. She wasn't so sure.

5

The Arrival

When the taxi pulled up to the townhouse, it was almost dark. The taxi driver flipped on the overhead light and touched the fare meter button.

"That'll be ninety bucks."

Nick stared at the meter.

"Ninety dollars?! The bus station was only four miles from here."

Looking annoyed, the driver sighed and began explaining the charges.

"As soon as we start the trip, the fare begins at $3.80. You started your trip during rush hour, so taxis charge double the fare. It's two of you, so that doubles that."

"You think I can't add? You're trying to rip us off!"

"I don't need to listen to this shit. Get out of my cab!"

Janice passed the man the money.

"Come on," she said while opening the door. "It's not worth it. Let's go."

Reluctantly, Nick climbed out.

"Pop the trunk," he growled as he walked to the back of the car to get their bags.

The trunk popped open, and Nick grabbed the bags.

"Fucking thief!" he yelled as he slammed the trunk shut.

As the two stood in the parking lot, Nick cursed the driver underneath his breath, watching the taxi leave. After looking around the neighborhood, his eyes lit up.

"Come on. It's that townhouse at the end of the sidewalk."

Nick grabbed the bags and started shuffling towards the townhouse. Janice paused to look at the place. Although the townhouses seemed bunched together, the homes were newer than the ones in her neighborhood. She marveled at the small squares of grass in front of each house.

"Is this what they call a front yard?" she asked as Nick knocked on the door.

"I guess. Most dogs probably wouldn't want to go on that."

After a few moments, the door swung open. A middle-aged woman wearing thick glasses stuck her head out.

"What do you want?" the woman asked rudely.

Nervously, Janice took a step back. The woman smelled like a cross between an old baked potato and dirty socks. Her curly blond hair had gray strands peppered throughout, and she wore thick bifocals that made her blue eyes look like moon pies.

"Are you Mrs. Staples?" asked Nick.

"Missus? I haven't been a missus for thirty years. Ever since I caught that no good son of a bitch in the bed with his secretary."

Janice shot a nervous look at Nick. Something wasn't right about the woman. Her words poured out of her mouth like a shaken soda – all in one continuous sentence with no space to breathe.

"Yeah, uh, Ms. Staples? We're here about the room?"

"Well, come on in and make yourself at home. The rent is due on the first. I hope you're clean, though. Those lazy bastards upstairs never pick up a broom. I guess I'll eat tuna and crackers for dinner."

The woman's continuous jumping from one subject to the next was confusing to Nick. Unsure of how he should respond, he spoke softly.

"Well...can you show us the room?"

"I told you to come in. Why are you still standing there? I need to pick up my package from the post office tomorrow."

Nick lifted the bag into the house and winked at his skeptical girl-friend. Janice was entirely out of breath from hearing the woman speak. Nothing she said made sense, and her words were all over the place.

As soon as they entered the house, Nick and Janice stopped and stared in disbelief. There were piles of magazines and newspapers every-where. Janice peeked into the kitchen, and her eyes widened. There were boxes of cereal on the counters, covering the floors, and even on the stove. Two large cats sat on the countertop, licking their paws as they stared at the new guests. The rank odor of spoiled milk shot into Janice's nose like ammonia, and she fought to stop herself from throwing up.

"Nick," Janice whispered.

But she couldn't finish the sentence. The disgusting smell was too strong, and Janice could only cover her nose and mouth to avoid vomit-ing. She pinched Nick's arm. Finally, he turned to her.

"What is it?" he whispered.

Janice nodded in the direction of the kitchen. He took one look and lowered his eyes.

"I know, baby," he whispered. "Just hold on."

Ms. Staples continued to speak without paying attention to the couple that entered her home. After a few seconds, she turned to face them and motioned the couple to follow her.

"You're on the bottom floor," Ms. Staples explained as she walked to the stairs. "No basement here, just three levels."

Suddenly the sound of male laughter interrupted the silence. Ms. Staples slapped the wall in anger and stuck her head over the railing leading to the upstairs floor.

"Shut the hell up, you! I tell you what. I'm going to kick that dumb son of a bitch out of here. He's already late on the rent. You have a private bathroom. I should charge you more money for it. Private bath-rooms are a luxury."

Finally, the trio reached the bottom of the stairs and turned down a poorly lit hallway. Ms. Staples stopped and handed Nick a set of keys.

"You're in that room at the end of the hall. Your bathroom is this room at the end of the hall. If you need groceries, you can go out and get them tomorrow. I need to clean out the fridge too, but my son's coming over. He'd better not ask me for any money because I'm broke. Deadbeat."

The woman left Janice and Nick standing in the dark hallway and returned upstairs. Nick opened the door and felt on the wall for a light switch.

"Holy crap!"

There were piles of magazines and clothing all over the room.

"We're supposed to live in this?" asked Janice after she saw the mess. "I can't do this, Nick."

"I didn't know about this crap," he said as he inched into the room.

"Maybe we should stay at a hotel tonight."

"We don't have money to waste."

"Have you paid her yet?"

"No."

"Don't. Let's get out of here, Nick. I'm scared."

"Look, let's just get some cleaning supplies from her and clean the room ourselves."

"Cleaning supplies? Look at this place. Do you think she can even spell the word *clean*?"

Nick frowned at his girlfriend and continued trying to navigate the room. Suddenly, he stopped.

"Hey! I think I found the bed!"

"Great."

"Come on, Janice. Let's try to make the best of this situation. I'm sure if she has soap and bleach, we can clean everything."

Nick returned to Janice and kissed her. Just as he was about to go down the dark hallway to return upstairs, he froze.

"Jesus!" he yelled.

There was a shadow standing at the end of the dark hallway.

"Ms. Staples is that you?" asked Nick.

The shadow stood motionless, breathing heavily. Curious about the reason for her boyfriend's cry, Janice stuck her head out of the room. She also saw the shadow at the end of the hallway and screamed.

"Aaaah! Nick! Is that her?"

Nick moved closer to Janice and grabbed her hand.

"Ms. Staples? Is that you?" he asked.

The woman mumbled incoherently and then responded.

"You got the rent money?" Ms. Staples asked as she walked closer. "It'll be $600 per month, and you have to pay it on time because I have my bills to pay too."

Janice pulled Nick back towards the light of the bedroom.

"Sure, we have the rent. You have a leasing agreement?"

"Leasing agreement?!"

The woman began muttering something underneath her breath.

"Goddamn it! I'll have it tomorrow."

"Then we'll have your money tomorrow."

Ms. Staples stomped her foot on the floor.

"Fine! Give me back my keys!"

"No problem," Nick replied. "Here you go."

Nick tossed the keys to the woman, and she walked toward the stairs. Before she left, she yelled down to them.

"Since you don't have the rent tonight, you need to leave," she growled.

"Okay," Nick replied.

He took Janice's hand and climbed the stairs to the front door. After grabbing their bags, they opened the door and walked outside. Janice sighed and turned to Nick.

"What are we supposed to do now?"

"There's nothing to it. There's a little convenience store at the end of the street. I'll just go and call another cab."

"And then what?"

Nick grabbed Janice and hugged her.

"Hey. Don't worry about this. We'll grab a hotel for the night. Tomorrow we'll come back with cleaning supplies and a small tv. It'll be okay."

"And you're sure about staying here?"

"The lady's a little off her rocker, but this is a nice community. I think I saw the subway when we were driving here. This place isn't so bad."

"I don't know. Doesn't the lady seem unstable? What if she's into drugs or something?"

"I doubt it. If Ms. Staples were into heavy drugs, there would be no way she'd be living here. She's just one of those hoarders, that's all."

Janice looked into Nick's eyes. The moonlight made them sparkle with determination and hope. Although their initial arrival made her afraid, she trusted him with all her soul. Maybe what they were experiencing was just a weird situation. She was sure they'd be able to adjust and overcome whatever problems they faced.

"Okay, Nick. Let's go before that crazy woman chases us away with a broomstick or something."

Nick smiled and kissed her on the lips.

"You see? That's why I love you. You're fearless."

"Fearless and hungry. Let's hurry and find a hotel before I die of starvation."

"Okay, we'll order some room service too."

"That sounds like a good plan."

Suddenly, Nick ran his tongue along her neck.

"And maybe later, dessert?"

Janice pushed him away and looked back at the house.

"Stop! She might see you!"

Janice was blushing, but she had to admit to herself that being alone with Nick had been in her mind for most of the trip. It had been so long since they were together.

Nick grabbed the bags, and the two of them walked into the night.

6

Checking in With Mom

It was almost one in the morning when Janice woke up. For a few seconds, she forgot where she was and became afraid. Suddenly a deep snore came from the pillow beside her, jolting her memory.

"Oh yeah. We're in a hotel," Janice whispered.

Suddenly, she remembered that they were both naked, and she moved closer to Nick. For her, sleeping in the nude was difficult. She could never get the right temperature that made her comfortable enough to go to sleep. The bedsheets felt course against her skin, and the thought of her boyfriend waking in the morning to see all the imperfections of her body made Janice uncomfortable.

After lying awake for several more minutes, Janice decided to get up and put on her bra and panties. The room was dark, and she could only see the light of the small alarm clock on the nightstand beside the bed. Instinctively, she climbed out of bed and walked over to the window to pull the curtains open.

"Janice?" asked Nick from the darkness.

Janice quickly grabbed her panties from the floor and slipped them on. Unable to find her bra, she turned away from the window as the city lights poured in.

"Shhhh...go back to sleep. I just need to go pee."

After mumbling something Janice couldn't understand, Nick started snoring again. Janice spotted her bra on the floor in front of the television. She grabbed it and quietly tiptoed to the bathroom. Once inside, Janice turned on the faucet in the sink and sat down on the toilet. Suddenly she began to smile. She couldn't believe she was in the big city with the love of her life. The whole two days seemed like a blur to her.

Janice flushed the toilet and stood to turn off the water faucet. Her eyes fell upon the telephone on the wall beside the door. Suddenly she felt nauseous. Thoughts of her parents crowded her mind: What were they doing? Did they call the police? How mad were they? Would they disown her? After looking at the phone receiver for several moments, Janice picked up the phone and dialed.

"Hello?"

"Mom?"

Janice's mother immediately started crying.

"Janice, how could you do something like this? Where are you?"

Janice could hear her stepfather in the background.

"Is it her? Where the hell is she?"

Janice ignored him and continued talking to her mother.

"Don't worry, Mom. I'm safe."

"What kind of girl does this? You run off in the night without telling your family where you're going? Who does that?"

"You would've said no."

"You're damned right I would've said no. You give up your family and your future to be with some boy? You know he sent his parents over here to run interference for him, don't you? What kind of man does that?"

"We decided on that because we were afraid you would call the cops."

"Your father *did* call the cops."

"You didn't stop him?"

"What did you expect us to do? You're kids! Babies in the wilderness. Do you think that boy's going to love you? Here's a hint, Janice. They all want sex. That's all you're suitable for at that age—just a quick lay. Men don't become mature until they're older. While they're young, they're no different than dogs."

"Nick is different, mom. He loves me."

"If he loved you so much, he wouldn't have come to your family's house to fuck you!"

Tears were streaming down Janice's face. She'd never heard her mother speak so harshly before. Suddenly, her stepfather snatched the phone from Janice's mother.

"Janice? Hey! Janice?"

"Yes, Michael. I'm here."

"You listen to me, and you listen good. You get yourself on the next bus home, and we won't take this thing any further. Everything will be forgiven and forgotten."

But Janice knew better. Her stepdad would probably have a shotgun or the police waiting for Nick as soon as they got home.

"No, Michael."

"What did you say?"

"Nick and I are staying."

Janice could hear the fury building in her stepfather's breathing. His voice suddenly started trembling as he talked.

"You tell that motherfucker if I catch him, I'm going to blow a hole in his fucking face!"

Janice lowered the phone from her ear and began sobbing. As she listened to her parents fighting for the phone, she regretted calling. Nick was right. It didn't make sense to call home.

"She just wants to act like a fucking slut. Let her! Good riddance!"

"Michael! I told you not to start! Now she'll never come home! Janice! Janice! Baby, can you hear me? Janice!"

Finally, Janice placed the phone back on her ear.

"Yes, mom. I'm here."

"Don't you worry about all of that tough talk from Michael. You get yourself on that bus and come home. Do you hear me?"

"No, Mom. Nick and I are seeing this through."

"What about your little brother Trevor? Are you just going to abandon him? He needs his sister!"

"That's not fair, mom."

"Come home and forget this foolishness. Your little brother needs you. We all need you!"

"Goodbye, mom."

"Janice, don't you hang up that phone. You get on…"

Janice hung up the phone and broke down crying. Her mother always knew what to say to tug at her heart. But this time, it wasn't going to work. She was with Nick, no matter the consequences.

After crying for a few minutes, Janice ran some cold water in the sink and washed her face. She walked out of the bathroom into the dark hotel room. Nick was lying on the bed with his arms behind his head. Janice climbed into bed beside him.

"That was pretty brutal, wasn't it?"

"About as bad as it gets, I guess. Your parents went to visit my parents. It didn't help. Now they're more pissed than ever."

"And your stepdad?"

"He threatened to come here and shoot you."

Nick got up from the bed and went to the loveseat sitting in front of the window.

"Come here," he whispered. "Sit with me for a moment."

Janice turned away from Nick and pulled the blankets up to her neck.

"I'm not in the mood, Nick. That phone call was bad. I never thought my mom would be so angry with me."

Refusing to accept her depression, Nick walked to the bed and grabbed Janice's arm.

"There's no way I'm letting your parents ruin our high. Come with me," he said as he tugged her arm.

Finally, Janice relented and walked to the chair with him. The two naked lovers sat on the chair and stared out into the city night.

"Do you see that?" asked Nick, pointing out into the city lights. "We're here chasing our dreams."

Janice looked out into the night sky and sighed. It would take more than a nice view of the city to raise her spirits.

"What if we made a mistake?" she asked.

Nick looked away from her.

"A mistake? Is that what you think this is? Is that what you think I am? A mistake?"

"You know that's not what I meant. But our families…"

"Our families are just that. Our families. Do you expect people raised 50 years ago to understand what drives a young heart?"

"No, but some things never change, Nick."

Nick took a deep breath and stared out into the city.

"You know what I see when I look out there?"

"No. What?"

"My future."

Janice looked out into the city and began to smile. Her boyfriend noticed her smile and nudged her.

"Come on. You can't tell me that you don't feel the excitement when you look out there. There's energy in this city. It's a special kind of energy reserved for those willing to acknowledge its existence. It's for the people that aren't afraid of letting go of pre-programmed notions of what their life is supposed to be."

Janice couldn't help feeling what Nick felt. There was no way she could chase her dreams back home. Not with a family like hers. Finally, Janice spoke.

"I'm here with you, baby."

"Are you sure? If you can't do it, let me know, and I'll purchase your ticket home."

Janice pushed her boyfriend in his chest.

"You would send me home? Really?"

"I can't force you to stay if your heart is at home. If you wanted to go, I wouldn't deny you."

Janice became angry.

"I thought you said you wanted to be with me forever, Nick!"

"I do. I mean…"

"People that want to spend the rest of their lives together don't talk about separation. Ever."

"Okay, baby. I'm sorry."

"And you'd better not ever repeat it. If you do, I will go home."

"Okay."

"Promise?"

Janice held up her pinky. Nick smiled and lifted his pinky finger.

"I promise."

Janice smiled and stood up.

"Good. Now come to bed and get to work."

"What?"

"You heard me. I want it."

Nick smiled.

"My pleasure, ma'am."

"Less talking and more fucking."

Nick kissed Janice, and they started making love again.

7

The Return to Crazy

The next day Nick and Janice checked out of the hotel and went to the nearest grocery store. After purchasing a money order and cleaning supplies, they stopped at a pawn shop to buy a small television and a portable refrigerator.

"We need to get sheets and blankets," instructed Janice.

Nick looked at her suspiciously.

"You're shopping like we have an endless supply of money. Besides, the place isn't even clean yet."

Janice pinched his cheeks.

"You see, that's why women are better planners than men. What are you going to sleep under when everything is clean? Your jacket?"

Nick laughed.

"I hadn't thought about that. You're right. Let's stop and pick up some linen."

The couple made a final stop at a department store. There, they purchased two sets of sheets and a blanket.

When they returned to the townhouse, Ms. Staples was sitting in front of the home, smoking a cigarette. When she saw the taxi drop the two off, she ran into the house and came out holding a paper and pen.

"You got the rent?" she asked without greeting the couple.

Nick extended his hand for the paper.

"Let's take a look at that lease first."

As Nick and Janice read the document, the old woman began rolling her eyes and impatiently sighing. Nick ignored her and continued reading until he finished.

"I guess it's okay," Nick said as he signed and passed it to his girlfriend.

After Janice finished reading and signing the paper, she dug into her purse and pulled out the money order.

"What the hell is this?" asked Ms. Staples when Janice gave her the check.

"It's a money order."

"Money order? I need the rent in cash, not a check. I can't do anything with that."

Nick was becoming frustrated and spoke up.

"Look. There isn't a single apartment in the whole city that wants cash instead of a cashier's check or money order. If you wanted cash, you should've told us that. But since you didn't, this is the payment method. Take it or leave it."

Ms. Staples turned and walked into the house. She mumbled something under her breath just as she had done before, but this time Nick and Janice heard it.

"Goddamned goodie-two-shoes country bastards."

Janice grabbed Nick's arm.

"Did you hear what she said?"

"Don't worry about it, baby. She's only complaining because she can't trick us."

When Ms. Staples came outside, she had keys in her hands. She thrust them to Nick.

"Here are your keys."

Still upset by what the woman said, Janice spoke up.

"You know, we heard what you said."

The woman looked surprised.

"What?"

"Yes. We heard what you said. That wasn't very nice."

"I don't know what you're talking about."

"Don't play stupid with me. You know exactly what you said."

Nick pulled at Janice's arm and whispered to her.

"Relax, baby. Let it go."

Ms. Staples stared at Janice for a few seconds and then walked past her into the parking lot.

"You have your keys. I need to go to the grocery store."

The woman climbed into her old pickup truck and sped away from the parking lot.

"That's one crazy lady," said Nick as he grabbed their belongings and went inside.

Janice shook her head in frustration and followed him.

8

House Cleaning

Janice and Nick spent the rest of the day cleaning out the room. After removing all the clutter and packing dozens of magazines in boxes, they sanitized every inch of the space.

"You know, this place isn't so bad," said Janice as she slapped a large sponge against the wall.

Nick agreed.

"I told you. It's not half bad. The lady is just too lazy to maintain it."

The more Nick and Janice cleaned, the more they liked the place. They discovered the room was much larger than they'd initially thought. The couple was thrilled that they'd have space to organize the room any way they wanted without compromising comfort.

"Thank God we have a bathroom at the end of the hallway just for us," said Janice. "I wouldn't want to share it with anyone."

"Me either," replied Nick. "And who knows? Maybe we can take some showers together."

Janice splashed water on him.

"Is that all you think about?"

"Well...mostly."

"Idiot."

The couple reorganized the room. Nick cleaned the mattress with soap and bleach and took it outside to dry in the sun while Janice scrubbed the ceiling, floors, and dresser. When they finished, the room looked better than the hotel they'd visited. Next, they tackled the bathroom. Although it wasn't as filthy as the bedroom had been, it had hard water stains, daddy long-leg spiders, and mildew. Nick and Janice scrubbed everything with soap and bleach, careful not to leave any area untouched. Janice had a phobia of spiders, and she put capfuls of bleach down the drain to be sure nothing could climb out to bite her when she was using the restroom.

By the time they finished cleaning everything, the sun was going down. Nick retrieved the mattress and fitted it with the sheets and blankets they'd purchased. Nick and Janice crashed on the floor.

"I can't believe we cleaned this whole place."

"Me either. But at least it's done now. You want to take your shower first?"

"No, Nick. You go first. There might be a spider in that bathroom."

"Wimp."

After Nick went to the bathroom, Janice turned on the television. There was nothing but white snow. Frustrated, she turned it off and sat on the edge of the bed. A sense of accomplishment washed over her. The two of them had made it into the big city. Now they only needed to chase their dreams.

Janice smiled as she heard Nick singing in the shower. He, too, must have felt a sense of accomplishment at what they had done. Nick ceased his singing and turned off the shower water. When she heard the bathroom door open, Janice grabbed her towel.

"Who are you?" asked Nick while tucking his towel around his waist.

Janice paused when she heard voices. Cautiously, she opened the door and looked into the hallway.

"Oh, hey. I thought I heard voices down here. Nancy told me I had a new housemate, so I came down to introduce myself. How are you? I'm Thomas."

Janice looked at the chubby guy in disgust. His bushy brown hair was oily, and his scruffy beard was unkempt. The once white t-shirt he was wearing wore the stains of several meals he'd consumed. The strange odor that crept down the hallway into Janice's nose told her that the man rarely bathed. His teeth were so yellow they looked like he'd bitten into a massive stick of butter.

"Thomas? Nice to meet you. Nancy? Is that Ms. Staples's first name?"

"Oh, yeah. Nancy is as nutty as squirrel shit, but she's not too bad."

"Good. Well..."

"What's your name?"

Suddenly Janice interrupted the two men talking.

"Nick?"

The man looked at Janice and smiled. Something about the way the man looked at her made Janice feel like she wasn't wearing clothes. She moved close to Nick and hid her body.

"This is your girlfriend? She's a beauty!"

Janice could tell that Nick was getting angry. He was very protective of her.

"Well, Thomas. As you can see, we're in the middle of getting settled here. We need to get cleaned up, and..."

"Oh, no problem. No problem. I just wanted to introduce myself. If you all need anything, just let me know."

As Thomas turned to go upstairs, he took another long glance at Janice before finally disappearing.

"The bathroom's all yours, babe," said Nick as he attempted to move past Janice into the bedroom. She grabbed him by the arm.

"Where do you think you're going?"

"To get dressed."

"No, you're not. There's no way I'm taking a shower and coming out into this dark hallway alone. Did you see the way he was staring at me? I felt like a piece of meat."

"Okay, okay. I'll go in with you under one condition."

Janice slapped Nick's arm.

"No! I can't be quiet during sex. You know that. No, Nick. Not now."

"Okay, but you have to let me shower with you. I couldn't clean my back properly. You don't want me climbing into bed all dirty, do you?"

Janice cracked a smile.

"Okay, but no funny business. Deal?"

"Deal."

The couple walked into the bathroom and locked the door.

9

Night Life

"Let's hit the club tonight!"

Janice looked at Nick as if he'd lost his mind. Although they had been in the city for over two weeks, she didn't feel comfortable going out.

"Are you serious? We don't even know our way around this city in the daytime, and now you want to go out at night? Are you crazy?"

"No, baby. I'm not crazy. We deserve it. For all the hard work we've done to get settled, we need to let off some steam."

"Nick..."

Janice was doubtful. Although they had learned so much about the city in the few days they were there, Washington, DC was still a giant concrete forest with many unfamiliar places.

"I can get a newspaper and look in their entertainment section. If all else fails, we can just ask the taxi driver."

"I don't know, Nick."

"Look. It doesn't have to be the most jumping club in the city. I want to see something with a live band. Maybe a rock club. I have to start chasing my dream at some point, you know?"

Janice considered Nick's point of view. The two of them came to the city to chase their dreams. At some point, they were going to need to make those dreams a reality. Although Janice was into paintings and art, Nick's goal of being a rock star wasn't any less important than hers.

"Okay. Let's go."

"Really?"

"Yeah. You're right. We need to start making things happen."

"Cool."

Nick headed to the shower singing loudly. Janice laughed at her silly boyfriend and turned her attention to what she would wear to the club.

It was midnight when they arrived at the club. A long line of people stood out from waiting to get in.

"Jesus, Nick. You said it was a small club. Is there a concert tonight?"

"The ad said live music. It didn't say anything about a concert."

Nick took some money from his pocket and paid the driver. As the couple exited the vehicle, Janice felt a sense of relief wash over her – the jeans she decided to wear turned out to be the necessary attire.

"Whoa," whispered Nick. "Some crowd."

"Yeah," Janice agreed.

To Janice, the whole line of people looked like they were all boarding a plane to mars. Each person seemed like they were doing their best to outdo the others for who was the weirdest. There were numerous people with strange facial piercings and colored contacts that made their eyes look funny. Some of the men had colorful mohawks, while a few of the women were completely bald. Janice tried to stop herself from staring by looking at the sidewalk, but she couldn't help casting the occasional open-mouthed glance. There was a seven-foot man dressed in a red curly wig that flowed to his feet. Janice could tell the man was trying to emulate his favorite heavy metal artist. Instead, he'd gone overboard – his shoulder pads and thick makeup made him look more like a clumsy electronic robot at an amusement park than a rock star. Two young girls that didn't seem to be older than 18 years old stood in line with very little clothing on - one had both her breasts exposed with only pasties covering her nipples, while the other looked like she had borrowed every color possible from her mother's makeup bag.

Finally, Nick and Janice made it to the back of the line. The wind was cooler than Janice expected, and she moved close to Nick for warmth. A large man wearing headphones walked up and down the line, pointing at people.

"You! Go," he yelled while motioning to an attractive blonde who was scantily dressed. The girl exited the line and walked to the entrance.

"Us! Let us in!" yelled the two young girls. The man stared at the girls suspiciously.

"How old are you?"

"Twenty-four."

The man started smiling.

"If you had said 21, I might've believed you. No way you're getting in here tonight."

Suddenly the girl with the nipple pasties extended her hand to the man – tucked inside her palm was a twenty-dollar bill.

"Can't you just let us in this time?" she asked. The man looked around to see if any of the patrons had noticed the exchange. Finally, he put the money in his pocket.

"No drinking and no fights. At the first sign of trouble, you're out on your ass."

"Oh, thank you! Come on, Chrissy!"

The two girls sprinted to the entrance of the club. Once again, a security guard stopped them from entering the club.

"Come on. That guy said we were cool," the girl said while pointing in the direction of the man they'd just paid.

"It's okay, Jeff. They're cool."

After seeing the girls run into the club, Nick called out to the guy with the headphones.

"Hey! Dude! Pssst!"

Janice became nervous.

"What are you doing, Nick?"

"Getting us into the club."

Nick reached into his pocket and pulled out a fifty-dollar-bill.

"You're going to give that guy fifty dollars? Are you nuts?"

"Well, I don't have boobs to flash, so money is our only option. Unless you're willing to…"

"Not on your life!"

The security guard walked up to Nick.

"You and you," he yelled to a couple near the front of the line. "Go in."

Nick extended his hand to the man.

"Hey, can you let us in?"

The man looked at the money and stuffed the fifty-dollar bill in his pocket.

"Hey, Jeff! Let these two go in!"

Janice and Nick hustled to the entrance. After being checked by security and getting a stamp placed on their hands, the couple entered the coat-check. The sounds of heavy metal music invaded their senses like loud police sirens. Janice couldn't understand the lyrics that the man was trying to sing. All she heard was the rattling of her brain as her eardrums begged for mercy.

"You hear that?" Nick yelled at her.

Janice could barely hear him.

"What?"

"I said, do you hear the music? This place is awesome!"

"If you say so!"

The couple walked through the curtains into the club. Like a wave of pain, the sounds of heavy metal ran up and down Janice's spine like a thousand needles. Suddenly a strange odor made itself noticed. It was a combination of alcohol, urine, cigarettes, and marijuana.

"Hey! You smell that?" she yelled at Nick.

"What?"

"I said, do you smell that?"

Nick raised his finger to his ear and mouthed that he couldn't hear her. He grabbed Janice's hand and pulled her behind him. The club was full, and there didn't seem to be a dance floor. Instead, a large group of people gathered in front of a stage. Many of the men looked like they were members of a motorcycle gang – their leather jackets and tattoos stood out like the strange jewelry that the people outside were wearing. Almost all of them had bottles of beer in their hands as they yelled at the performers.

"Nick!" yelled Janice.

He didn't hear her and continued pushing ahead.

"Nick!" she yelled again.

This time Janice yanked on his arm. When he turned around, she pulled him close and screamed into his ear.

"Let's go to the bar!"

Nick looked at the stage before finally shaking his head in agreement. Janice was no fool. The mixture of alcohol and testosterone was sure to cause a fight. She didn't want to be anywhere near them when the explosion occurred.

As the couple moved towards the bar sitting on the right side of the room, Nick accidentally bumped into a woman.

"Hey! Why don't you watch where the fuck you're going?" the woman barked.

Nick touched the woman on the arm.

"I'm sorry. I was trying to…"

"Don't you fucking touch me, you fucking douchebag! Go back to Hicksville or wherever you two squares are from."

Suddenly, a large musclebound man appeared behind the woman.

"We have a problem here?" the man asked while opening his leather jacket.

Tucked into his waist was the handle of a knife. Janice saw the weapon and pulled her boyfriend back.

"Nick," Janice said nervously. After seeing the knife, Nick attempted to diffuse the situation.

"Look, man, I don't have a problem. I just bumped into your girl-friend by accident. Why don't you let us buy you guys a couple of beers, and let's let bygones be bygones, okay?"

"Fuck your fucking beer. You back-alley-hick! Just stay the fuck out of our way!"

The girl pushed past Nick and stormed away into the crowd. Her boyfriend glared at Nick and Janice for a few seconds and then followed. Nick grabbed Janice's hand.

10

Everyone Knows

"Maybe we should just sit by the bar for a little while," he yelled.

The two moved to the two available stools at the bar, and Nick ordered two beers. Janice noticed the female bartender staring at them as she served their drinks. Nick leaned close to Janice and spoke loudly into her ear.

"What do you think so far?"

"You mean about almost getting stabbed to death?"

"Forget that. What do you think about the club?"

"The music's too loud, and the people are weird. I'd rather we stayed home."

"Oh, don't be so nervous. We just need to learn the city a little more."

"I'm ready to go."

Frustrated, Nick gulped his beer and looked at the group performing on stage.

"Wait here. I'm going to see if I can talk to one of the band members."

"About what?"

"Performing. I don't know."

Nick drank a final sip of his beer and went through the crowd.

"You guys are lucky," the female bartender exclaimed as she lifted Nick's glass and wiped the bar.

Janice took a sip of her beer and looked at the redhead as she wiped the counter.

"Excuse me?"

"That guy you almost got into a fight with is serious trouble."

"Really?"

"Yeah. That dude stabbed someone a few months back."

"How is he still here? Shouldn't he be in jail or something?"

"His friend owns this place. It's mostly about who you know in DC. Where are you from?"

"Charleston."

"I knew you guys weren't from around here."

"Yeah? How did you know?"

"Truthfully? Your hairstyle. It's not one that the people wear."

Janice touched her hair and looked around to see if anyone noticed. She didn't know if she should be offended or not.

"Oh, don't worry about it. Your hair is fine. It's just different than the colored hair and mohawks in this place. By the way, my name is Scarlett."

The bartender extended her hand to Janice.

"Hi Scarlett, I'm Janice. How long have you been bartending here?"

"I've been here for about one year."

"You must see a lot of wild stuff."

"Yeah, things can get pretty crazy."

"How do you keep all the men from acting like jerks?"

"Most of the guys here care more about alcohol than getting a piece of ass. Plus, it helps that anytime someone steps out of line, I can call security to toss them out."

"It's as simple as that?"

"For the most part, yeah. I did have a guy grab my ass one time, but the beatdown he received from security was so bad he didn't even come back to the club."

"Jesus."

"Yeah, people tend to remember getting their face turned to hamburger meat."

Janice finished her drink and pushed the mug away.

"You want another?"
"I'd better not. We're on a budget."
"No worries. This one's on the house."

11

Calling it a Night

By the time Nick made it back to the bar, Janice had almost finished her third beer. By her standards, she was drunk, and there would be no way she would be able to leave the club without her boyfriend's assistance. Janice and the bartender were talking the whole time Nick was gone. Janice discovered that Scarlett was originally from Virginia and had moved to the city only two years ago. She was engaged to a truck driver that spent more time on the road than she liked, and they planned to get married during Christmas.

"Hey!" Nick yelled as he hopped onto the barstool, almost sliding onto the floor.

"Nick, are you drunk?" asked Janice.

"Those guys are fucking awesome!" Nick continued. "Awesome, I tell you!"

Janice started giggling uncontrollably and knocked her empty glass down.

"Are you two going to be okay?" asked the bartender.

Janice smiled and waved her off.

"I'll be fine. We just need to get this boy home," she said as she reached out to Nick.

"Yeah, we know what you want when we get home," Nick said through slurred words.

"And you better be able to last this time," replied Janice. "No more of that weak shit."

The bartender burst out laughing.

"You guys are cute, but you'd better get home."

"Oh, I'm not that drunk. Nick is drunker than I am."

Nick smiled and shook his head in agreement.

"I'm fucking toasted!"

"Well, regardless, the bar is closed now. Do you need me to call you a taxi?"

Nick stuck his tongue in Janice's mouth, and they both started kissing and groping one another passionately. The bartender picked up the phone.

"Okay. I'll take that as a yes."

After dialing the taxi, Scarlett called over security.

"David, these are a couple of friends of mine. I called a taxi for them. Make sure they get in, okay?"

"Sure thing, Scarlett."

The security guard led the couple to the taxi sitting in front of the club. They climbed in, and Janice gave the driver the address. After the cab had been driving for a few minutes, Nick punched the car seat.

"Shit!"

"What is it? What's wrong?"

"I forgot my jacket."

Janice forgot she wore a jacket to the club too.

"We'll get them. I'll call Scarlett tomorrow and tell her to hold them."

"Scarlett? Who the fuck is Scarlett?"

"The bartender, dummy."

"Oh."

Nick closed his eyes and laid his head on the seat. Within seconds he was snoring. Although Janice was drunk, her fear of the city kept her eyes open. As she looked out of the car window at the city lights, she wondered what her family was doing. Were they worried about her? What new tricks had her little brother learned since she was gone? Did he miss his older sister? Was her dad on his way to crash into her world and take her home by force?

By the time the taxi pulled up in front of their townhouse, Janice's eyelids were heavy with sleep.

"Nick...Nick...we're home," Janice said as she pushed her sleeping boyfriend.

Nick moaned a little and continued sleeping. Janice paid the taxi driver and went around to the other side of the car to retrieve her boyfriend. After yanking on him for a few moments, Nick staggered out of the car into her arms.

"Gosh, Nick. What did you drink?" Janice asked as she held him up.

Nick mumbled something and started laughing uncontrollably. Janice looked at his eyes and became nervous. His eyes were completely bloodshot. He placed his arm around her neck and led him to the front door of the house. After fumbling with the keys, she managed to unlock the door. As she pushed the front door open, Nick took one step and fell on the floor.

"Nick! What the hell did you drink?" Janice whispered.

Suddenly the lights in the house came on.

"Hey! Is everything okay down there?" asked a male voice from upstairs.

Janice lifted Nick to his feet and walked to the stairs leading down to their room. Just as she was about to descend, she heard someone coming down the stairs above her. It was the disgusting roommate, Thomas.

"Here, let me give you a hand," the man said.

Janice pressed her face against Nick and tried to lift him on her own. She didn't want anything to do with Thomas. He smelled like spoiled bologna.

Nick mumbled a little, and his legs gave out. Just as he was about to fall down the stairs, Thomas swooped in underneath his armpit and lifted him.

"I'm sorry," said Janice. "I didn't know he was this out of it."

"That's alright. We all need to blow off steam sometimes. It looks like Nick had a good time tonight."

Janice remained silent. She didn't want to build any type of rapport with Thomas. Something about the guy creeped her out. Finally, the trio reached the bottom of the stairs and navigated through the dark hallway until they reached Janice's and Nick's bedroom. After unlocking the door and turning on the lights, they guided Nick to the bed and laid him down.

"He's a lot heavier than he looks," said Thomas while breathing heavily.

"Yeah, well, thanks for the help," replied Janice.

She walked to the bedroom door and held it open for the man to leave.

"You know, you have some gorgeous eyes. Some of the most pretty I've ever seen."

Janice looked at Nick lying on the bed, hoping he would wake up. She didn't want to make eye contact with Thomas under any circumstances. She could feel his eyes crawling up and down her body.

"Look, we need to get some rest. We've had a busy day, you know?"

"Sure. Of course. Hey, do you want me to go into the bathroom and get the shower started for you? I could do that, you know?"

"Um, no, thank you. My boyfriend can handle that."

Thomas moved closer to Janice.

"There isn't a whole lot Nick can do for you while he's passed out like that. I could help you out, you know. While he's out of it..."

Janice backed away.

"Look, Thomas, I want to sleep. Goodnight. Okay?"

"It could be a *really* good night. Do you know what I'm saying? Let me help you out a little."

Suddenly, Nick stirred and turned over. Thomas quickly stepped away from Janice.

"I see you guys have everything under control now," he said as he walked out of the room. "Goodnight."

As soon as the man was gone, Janice ran to the door and locked it. She laid down on the bed beside her boyfriend and kicked off her shoes. There was no way Janice was going to shower with that guy lurking around the house. In time, she fell asleep.

12

Disgusting Things at The Ungodly Hour

"Baby, I need to throw up."

Janice sat up suddenly in bed and looked at Nick. The expression on his face told her that he was about to blow.

"Go to the bathroom," Janice yelled as she struggled to move out of the way.

It was too late. Like a volcano, orange chunks of vomit spewed from his mouth and splashed on Janice's chest and legs.

"Shit!" she screamed.

Nick opened the bedroom door and took off running down the hall, vomiting with each step he took. Janice stripped all the sheets from the bed and put them into a garbage bag. Trying to ignore the putrid smell that filled the room, she took off all her clothes and stuffed them into the same bag.

"Oh God!" whispered Nick between fits of vomiting into the toilet.

Janice wanted to go to the bathroom to check on him, but she was too disgusted. After wiping the vomit off her legs, Janice removed one of Nick's t-shirts from the drawer and put it on. She pulled a bucket from the closet, filled it with disinfectant, and walked to the bathroom.

"Baby are you okay?" she asked as she peered into the bathroom.

Nick was a mess. He sat on the floor half-asleep, clutching the toilet with vomit on the side of his face.

"I'll be okay. Don't worry..."

Janice placed the bucket into the shower and filled it up with hot water.

"Nick, go ahead and climb into the shower."

"I...don't feel like it."

"Do it. You can't get in bed with vomit all over you."

"Just let me sleep here on the floor."

"No, Nick. You'll feel a lot better after you've showered. Come on now."

Janice turned on the shower and helped Nick to get in. After waiting a few minutes, she carried the mop bucket into the room and started cleaning up. Within a few minutes, she finished cleaning. Nick stumbled back to the bedroom naked but smelling considerably better.

"You look better."

"Yeah, that shower helped me. I think I'm probably going to sleep for most of the day tomorrow."

"It's probably a good idea. What exactly did you have to drink at the club?"

"Huh?"

"What did you drink?"

"Oh. The band had a bottle of homemade whiskey. I guess it was too strong for me."

"I guess so."

Nick flopped down on the freshly cleaned bed.

"Come lay down with me."

"I'd better get into the shower myself. The smell of your vomit is on everything."

Nick sat up and picked up the bag of dirty laundry.

"Give me your clothes and climb into the shower. I'll take this to the laundry room and get a load started."

"At 3 in the morning?"

"Sure. Why not? Everyone's probably dead to the world."

Janice took off her clothes and handed them to Nick. After peeking out the bedroom door, she ran down the hallway to the bathroom and turned on the shower.

As she stood in the shower letting the water massage her face, Janice finally noticed the pounding headache she had at the top of her head. She forgot that she'd drank those beers, and she was paying the price. The smell of Nick's vomit was still everywhere, so Janice decided to wash her hair. Doing that made her headache more intense, and she began to get dizzy. The headache seemed to make everything move in slow motion. Finally, Janice finished showering and climbed out.

"Shit!" Janice whispered.

She forgot that Nick had taken the last towel to the room. Janice opened the door of the bathroom and walked out into the dark hall. Janice didn't know why, but she felt something strange crawling up her spine. Suddenly her whole body filled with goosebumps, and she began trembling.

Slowly, she turned around.

Standing at the end of the hallway was a shadow. Janice knew who it was - it was Thomas! His pants were down around his ankles, and he was moving his hand rapidly back and forth.

"Oh my God!" yelled Janice.

She took off running to her bedroom, slammed the door, and locked it. Nick was asleep on the bed, snoring.

"Nick! Nick!" she whispered. "Thomas was watching me coming out of the bathroom!"

Her boyfriend's only response was snoring. Janice took a fresh towel out of the drawer and dried herself off. Afraid to turn off the light, she slid into the bed beside him and kept the lights on. Janice stared at the door expecting the pervert to enter. Eventually, she fell asleep.

13

The Truth Always Comes Out

"He did what?"

"Yeah. While you were sleeping, Thomas stood outside the bathroom and jerked off while I went to the room."

"Are you sure?"

"I saw his shadow. I know it was him."

"You didn't see his face?"

"I didn't need to. It was Thomas."

"Wait. Was he looking in the bathroom?"

"No. I came out without a towel because..."

"What?! You came out naked?!"

"You took the towel, and there was no way for me to yell for you to bring another one. You were sleeping."

"I mean, I was going to kick his ass, but now? How can I get mad at a guy that saw my girlfriend walking around the house without wearing clothes? He didn't make you get naked. Hell, he didn't even peek in the bathroom."

"What?! You think this is my fault?!"

"No...not exactly, but..."

"Then what are you saying, Nick? You're going to allow another man to jerk off in front of me and blame me for it?"

"What do you want me to do?"

"You can do whatever you want. But I'm moving out of here today!"

"But we signed a lease. I can't just break it."

"I think psycho pervert qualifies as a reason to break the lease."

"Wait here. I'll be back."

Nick stormed out of the room and stomped up the stairs. Janice sat down on the bed and listened as he yelled for Thomas throughout the house. After a few minutes, Nick returned to the room.

"He's not here."

"So..."

"So, we wait until he returns."

Janice grabbed her luggage and started putting her clothes inside.

"You wait. I'm gone."

Nick slammed the suitcase closed.

"You can't leave, Janice. That's not how it works. We're in this together."

Janice kicked the luggage onto the floor.

"We leave today, or I'm going home!"

"Home?"

"I can't stay in a place where I don't feel safe!"

Nick grabbed the luggage from the floor and tossed it on the bed. Afterward, he grabbed his bag and started stuffing his clothes inside.

"I don't know how we're going to get out of this one. We just forfeit our deposit and move again. I can't believe this shit!"

Although Janice hated threatening Nick, it was the only tool available to get him to do the right thing. She packed her bags quietly and listened to him rant about how much money they were going to lose. But Janice didn't care. The only thing she wanted was to get rid of the freak.

When they had finished packing their clothes, Nick and Janice carried their bags up the stairs. Just as they opened the door, Thomas stood with his key out about to place it in the lock. Nick took one look at him and exploded. Nick punched Thomas so hard that he fell backward onto the sidewalk. Janice ran out of the door and stood watching, a sense of satisfaction coursing through her. She didn't feel an ounce of sympathy for the man.

"Hey! What are you hitting me for?" Thomas asked while lying on the ground.

Nick kicked him in the stomach.

"Pervert, son of a bitch! That's for jacking off in front of my girl!"

"I wasn't even here last night!"

Nick delivered a more violent kick to Thomas's ribs.

"Who said it happened last night, you sick fuck? You told on yourself!"

Janice moved closer to Thomas.

"You were there!" she yelled.

Nick grabbed the man by the collar of his shirt and delivered one final blow to the man's nose. Blood splashed everywhere.

"Here's a piece of advice. Get a porn collection and stay the fuck away from women. If you keep this up, someone's going to kill you."

Just as Nick delivered one final kick to Thomas's back, Ms. Staples's car pulled into her parking space. She climbed out and immediately started yelling.

"Hey! What the hell is going on here?"

Nick and Janice grabbed their bags and walked away from the house.

"Why don't you ask Mr. Pervert?" replied Nick. Ms. Staples glared at him.

"I knew you were nothing but trouble."

"Me?"

"Yeah, you! That southern charm was always a disguise. I knew you would be a handful."

Suddenly, Janice jumped in.

"Nick didn't do anything. It's this sick idiot that's the guilty one!"

"What are you talking about?"

"He saw me coming out of the bathroom and started masturbating in front of me!"

Ms. Staples's eyes widened as she looked at Janice in disbelief. She started shaking her head.

"No. You're mistaken."

"She's not!" yelled Nick. "That dummy's a pervert!"

The woman went to Thomas's side and grabbed him by the arm.

"Get up," she said.

"It's not true. I swear!" said Thomas as he wiped his bloody nose with the sleeve of his shirt.

"I don't believe them," whispered Ms. Staples. "Don't worry."

Janice looked around. A group of nosey neighbors had gathered to watch the confrontation.

"You couldn't have done it. We had sex last night. I'm your nasty baby, aren't I?" whispered Ms. Staples.

Nick and Janice stood with mouths open as Ms. Staples's words started tumbling out in bunches. She seemed intent on convincing herself that the incident didn't happen and that the disgusting man was in love with her.

"It didn't happen. Of course, it didn't. You wouldn't hurt me, would you? I know you. These two are just trouble. You love me, I know. Yeah? Of course, you do. I do so many nasty things for you. Just the way you like it. Good nasty, right? Of course. I'm your everything. They're just making stuff up."

Janice couldn't hold her tongue any longer.

"Damn! You're a couple of sick fucks!" she exclaimed. "No wonder you're defending him."

"Just clear out your room and get out of here!" barked the woman as she helped Thomas to the house.

"We're already packed," yelled Nick.

"Good! If you're not out of here in 30 minutes, I'm calling the police."

Nick picked up both bags, and he and Janice started their walk to the convenience store to call a taxi.

14

The New Repeat

Janice had just taken a bite of her hamburger when Nick lifted her chin and kissed her on the lips.

"Sorry, babe."

"For what?"

"For not listening to you. I always knew Ms. Staples was weird, but I didn't think it was anything crazy. Boy, was I wrong."

"I don't care about that, Nick. Let's just make a promise to always listen to one another. If there's a situation that makes you or me feel uncomfortable, we need to always listen to one another."

Nick took a huge bite of his burger and shook his head.

"Agreed."

"What are we going to do now?"

"I guess we'll stay in this hotel for about three days and try to find an apartment."

"An apartment? But won't that eat into our budget?"

"For sure. But we don't have a choice now. We need space, and we need privacy."

"Isn't that the truth."

"Tomorrow, I'll go out and get us a cell phone. After that, we start combing the city for cheap apartments. And we also start our job searches."

"Jobs?"

"Yeah. Our savings are disappearing quickly. We have to find a way to get some income coming in. Flipping burgers, cashier. I don't care. We have to get some money."

Janice took another bite of her burger and stared at Nick with concern. The reality of their decision to move finally hit her, and she almost wished she hadn't been so spontaneous with leaving the rented room. Suddenly an idea entered her head.

"Should we call our families to help us?"

"What?"

"There's no telling how long this job search is going to take us. It could be months before we find something."

"I can hear my father now. 'Real men don't call their parents for money,' he'd say. And can you imagine what your parents are going to say?"

Janice thought about her dad. There would be no way in hell she'd be able to get in a word with him after she asked for money.

"Maybe that's not such a good idea."

"Yeah, maybe not."

Janice and Nick spent the rest of the evening watching movies and plotting out what they were going to do for the week. They agreed that she would be the one to focus primarily on the job search. The hotel had an office set up for the guests, including a row of computers, a fax machine, and a copier. She could work on both their resumes and submit them to potential employers. Meanwhile, Nick was going to check out apartments. While they both agreed that their budget was limited, Nick promised Janice that he would look for apartment communities that were clean, safe, and as close to their asking price as they could get. Nick didn't return to the hotel until 8 in the evening.

"You must've seen a lot of apartments," Janice exclaimed, frustrated by his absence.

"Oh, I saw quite a few apartments, but t-t-they were out of our budget."

"Where are all the flyers and apartment plans? I know they give you those things when you go to view apartments?"

"Oh…I didn't save those. It didn't make s-s-sense. We couldn't afford those places."

Janice was suspicious now. Nick smelled of beer, and his words were slurring.

"Where exactly did you go?"

"I went looking for apartments. Oh! Remember that band we saw at the club?"

"I never saw anyone. You did."

"Yeah, well, I bumped into the guy on the train. It turns out they're looking for someone on lead guitar. I told them I'd go check them out this weekend."

"Nick…"

"What? Can't I work on my dream in my spare time? I spent all day looking at apartments we can't afford. Shouldn't I be networking a little? The guy could've known about some cheap apartments."

"Well…did he?"

"What?"

Janice turned away from Nick and flipped through the stack of resumes she'd printed out. She wanted to yell at Nick because of his irresponsible behavior. She'd spent all day calling companies inquiring about available jobs and setting up interviews. The least Nick could do was take the apartment search seriously.

"Hey. Tomorrow I'm going to meet up with," said Nick while stumbling into the bathroom.

Janice couldn't restrain herself.

"What? We have to find jobs and a place to live! How are we supposed to do that if you're out running around with your friends?"

"Relax. Calm down. I was going to meet up with the band tomorrow night."

"And you think you should be doing this if we don't have a place to live?"

"We'll be okay."

"We will? How much money do we have left?"

"Um...I'm not sure."

"You see? You're out here acting like we have an endless supply of money, and we don't! We have approximately $2,325 left before all hell breaks loose."

Nick came out of the bathroom and stumbled over to Janice. He wrapped his arms around her waist and attempted to kiss her. She moved away in disgust. His breath stunk of alcohol.

"Don't touch me, Nick. I don't like it when you're like this."

"What? You don't love me anymore?"

Janice pushed him away a final time and went into the bathroom.

"I need to shower," Janice said as she slammed the door.

She climbed into the shower and let the water splash on her face. Nick's behavior was changing, and she didn't know how to feel about it. Maybe her parents were right about him. Maybe Nick was too irresponsible to take on such a big task as relocating to the city. There was no question that her boyfriend was more than a little careless.

"Maybe I'm just overreacting," she whispered.

After all, Nick was enduring the same hardships as she was. He hadn't done anything but try to extend himself to make a few friends.

"I probably just need to get laid," Janice said as she washed her hair.

After showering, Janice dried herself off and blow-dried her hair. She brushed her teeth and rubbed her body with the cherry blossom lotion Nick had given her before they came to the city. She sprayed her most delicious perfume and was about to put on her underclothes when she decided not to.

"I'm getting laid tonight," she whispered as she opened the bathroom door.

When Janice walked into the hotel room, Nick lay slumped over on the couch, snoring. The sight was like ice to Janice's burning desire. Sexually frustrated, she climbed into bed and went to sleep.

15

Determined

Janice got up early the next day, put on her most professional attire with her high heel shoes, and prepared to go out into the city to find a job. After showering and getting dressed, Janice looked over at Nick, still snoring in bed.

"If you don't get your ass out on that street today…" she mumbled beneath her breath.

Janice thought about spoiling Nick's morning by waking him up with the alarm clock's loud music, but she hesitated. She didn't want Nick to blame her for starting his morning off on a sour note. Still, after applying her makeup, Nick was sleeping without a care in the world. Janice got pissed off. She grabbed her stack of resumes from the desk, opened the hotel door, and slammed it rudely behind her – to intentionally wake Nick.

"Hey! What the…" Janice heard her boyfriend yell as she walked quickly down the hall with a wicked grin on her face.

It was time for Nick to get off his lazy ass and get moving.

Janice canvassed all the places within walking distance of the hotel and filled out a few applications from the newspaper's employment section - a thrift store, a law office, and a dental office. Eventually, she found her way to the closest shopping mall. After snacking on a cheeseburger in the food court, Janice walked through the mall, submitting applications to all the stores. Most of the store workers greeted her with the suspicion that most gave someone her age – a skeptical look as they took her resume and gave her the "we'll be in touch" response, while others were too busy to even look in her direction. Still, Janice's determination pushed her on to store after store. By the time she made it back to the hotel, her ankles hurt so severely that Janice thought she had sprained her ankles. After entering the hotel room and finding Nick wasn't there (she wasn't surprised at all), Janice flopped down at the cheap desk and counted all the places she'd applied for employment.

"No way," Janice said as she finished counting everything.

She'd applied to twenty-three different stores! Proud of her accomplishments, Janice grabbed a bag of potato chips from the counter, kicked off her shoes, and turned on the television to watch some daytime talk shows. Just as she did, Nick entered the hotel.

"Hey babe," he said as he sat down on the edge of the bed. Janice ignored his greeting and got right to the point.

"How did it go?"

"You still mad at me, huh?"

"I'm not mad. How did it go?"

"It went okay?"

"Just okay? We're running out of money fast."

Nick stood up and pulled off his shirt.

"You worry too much, baby."

Janice wanted to explode when she heard Nick's comment. Instead, she ignored him, grabbed the television remote, and turned the channel. She watched as Nick walked into the bathroom and started peeing without closing the door. Janice was becoming sick of his shit. After he finished urinating, Nick washed his hands and walked out of the bathroom. He opened the luggage and pulled out a fresh shirt.

"You ready to go?"

"Where, to meet your friends? I don't think so."

"It's not to meet them. We could go out and have a light dinner somewhere. Just the two of us."

"Dinner?! Are you fucking..."

Janice stormed into the bathroom and slammed the door. Nick walked to the bathroom door and spoke to her.

"Relax, baby. You're getting yourself worked up over nothing."

"Don't talk to me, Nick. I don't have the patience right now."

"But why?"

Suddenly Janice snatched open the door.

"Why?! Are you fucking serious?"

"But I was going to tell you that..."

"How much of our money did you spend today on drinking?"

"What?"

"You hooked up with your new friends again, right?"

"No."

"Then tell me this, Nick. What the hell are we supposed to do? Live in his hotel until we're sitting on zero? A couple of more days and..."

Nick walked over to the desk and pushed everything onto the floor.

"Stop!" he yelled.

Janice stared at him with wide eyes, unsure of how to react to his sudden output of violent behavior.

"Just shut the fuck up for two minutes! Please!"

He dug into his back pocket and pulled out a stack of folded papers. Angrily, he threw them on the desk.

"What are those?"

"It's what you've been bitching about for the past two days. A lease!"

"But how?"

"I'm unemployed, so I knew most people wouldn't give me the time of day. So, I did what anyone in our position would've done. I lied."

Janice picked up the papers and started reading them.

"It's a studio apartment. It's only us, so I figured that space was irrelevant for the time being. We just needed to find a place to lay our heads until we get on our feet."

"How much is it?"

"$800 per month with utilities included. With what we have left, I figure this gives us two months to find jobs before things fall apart."

Janice jumped into Nick's arms.

"I'm so proud of you! I knew you could do it!"

Nick blushed and looked away.

"Not without you damn near killing me every day until it happened."

Janice was so excited. Her mind was a ball of energy.

"I applied to 23 jobs today."

"Really?"

"At this rate, I should have a job by the end of the week. The only thing we need to worry about now is finding you a job."

"That shouldn't be too difficult now that we have a place to sleep."

"Were you still going to meet those guys tonight?"

"Actually, I was going to take you out in celebration of the new place."

"That sounds great, honey. Just let me take a shower. I've been stomping around like Frankenstein in those damned high heels all day."

"Okay. I'll shower too. Then we'll go out and grab something cheap to eat."

Janice kissed Nick and headed into the bathroom. As she stripped down to shower, she stopped and smiled at her reflection in the mirror. Things were finally looking up for the two of them. She felt so happy she felt like calling her mother to tell her the news. She immediately decided against it. Janice's mother would do nothing but complain and would probably ruin the moment for them. She turned on the hot water and watched her face slowly disappear in the steam on the mirror.

"I guess this is goodbye to the old me," she whispered as the mirror fogged.

She climbed into the shower and prepared for her celebration with her boyfriend.

16

Onward

The next day Nick and Janice got up early and checked out of the hotel. The hotel clerk was friendly and allowed them to leave their luggage there for a few hours while they went to sign the lease for their new apartment. They took the subway four stops away and got off at a large apartment complex.

"The main office is over there," said Nick as he pointed in the direction of a large building with dozens of flags surrounding it.

Janice pulled on Nick's arm and gave him a massive kiss on his cheek.

"I'm so excited," she exclaimed as they walked to the office.

Now they'd be able to call their parents without shame. Signing the contract would make everything official. They would no longer be visitors to the city; they'd be residents. Janice and Nick belonged, and no one would be able to tell them otherwise.

"Just married, right?" asked the overweight rental agent as he sat down and placed the papers before the excited couple.

"We're not married yet, but we're planning," lied Nick.

The agent smiled and went over the details of the rental.

As Nick signed the contract, Janice noticed that his hand was shaking. She patted his leg and tried to comfort him without the agent noticing. Although he'd pissed her off with his procrastination, Nick came through in the end, and that's all Janice wanted.

"Congratulations," said the agent as he gave Janice the keys. "You can move in whenever you're ready."

The happy couple stood up, shook the agent's hand, and walked out of the building. After searching the surrounding buildings, they finally located theirs – the oldest building at the back of the lot.

"That's our building? It looks so old," complained Janice.

"Well, it's all we could afford. Besides, we don't even have jobs. We couldn't get the most expensive apartment," replied Nick.

"But it looks pretty old."

"Come on, let's try to be more positive."

The apartment was a lot smaller than Janice thought it would be. She'd never seen a studio apartment, and in her mind, she imagined a big airy room atop an industrial building. Instead, what they got was a small, cramped room no larger than a few hundred feet on the ground floor of an apartment building that seemed to be a thousand years old. There was a stove in it that looked so ancient that Janice guessed it was from the '70s. The fact that the contraption was gas frightened Janice even more. She imagined going to make a cup of tea and having the whole apartment explode.

The other parts of the apartment were even more alarming. There was one closet that Janice and Nick would have to share. It was only large enough to hang half of her suitcase full of clothes, let alone her boyfriend's. The bathroom didn't offer much comfort either. The toilet was so close to the shower that it was almost inside it. The sink was old with dark brown water stains, and the bathroom floor had a hole in it close to the toilet. Janice worried that it would fall through the floor if she sat on it, and the police would find her naked in the next apartment covered in toilet water.

"Nick..."

"I know. I know. It's just the beginning, babe. We'll get something new when we both get jobs."

Suddenly a buzz came from Nick's pocket. It was the cell phone they recently purchased. Nick flipped the phone open and answered it.

"Hello? Yes. Yes, ma'am. She's right here."

Nick passed Janice the phone.

"It's for you. It sounds like a job."

Janice took the phone and walked to the far side of the room.

"This is Janice."

"Hi, Janice. My name is Julie Winters. I'm the hiring manager at Corner Books. You applied for a job with us."

"Yes."

"We're wondering if you'd be available to start tomorrow."

"Really? No interview?"

"Well, I'll be honest. We've had to make a sudden staff change that leaves us at a disadvantage."

"I see."

"After reviewing your resume, we think you'd be a good fit. You interested?"

"Sure."

"It's a basic sales position with pay starting at $11.75 an hour. You'll be a full-time employee, and you'll get two days off per week."

"Sounds good."

"Okay, so we'll see you tomorrow at 9?"

"Absolutely."

"Wear jeans tomorrow, and we'll give you a few company shirts when you arrive."

"Great!"

"See you tomorrow."

"Goodbye."

Janice ran over to Nick and hopped on his back, pushing him face-first into the wall.

"I got a job! I got a job!" she screamed.

Nick bounced off the wall and fell to the floor.

"Damn, baby. Don't give me a concussion."

"Now you have to get a job."

"Cool. When do you start?"

"Tomorrow. Can you believe it?"

"That's awesome."

Janice climbed on top of Nick's chest and kissed his face.

"I guess we're not going home after all."

"I guess not."

"Tomorrow, while I'm at work, you can go and do what I did. Hit the mall and drop applications everywhere."

Nick kissed Janice once more and raised himself from the floor and opened the front door.

"Come on. We need to go get our luggage and stop off at the store to buy a few things."

17

Closer to the Dream

"Are you coming with me to the club tonight?"

Janice kicked off her shoes and flopped down on the bed.

"The club? I have to work tomorrow, and you do too. I don't think either of us should be going to the club when we have to get up early."

"You're such an old woman."

"You've called me that before, and it doesn't bother me."

"Okay, but don't complain when some hot girl tries to talk to me."

Janice looked at Nick and tilted her head in curiosity.

"Is that what we're doing now?"

"What?"

"Inspiration through jealousy?"

Nick smiled.

"Is it working?"

"Maybe a little. Let me take a shower and get dressed."

As the taxi wound through the city and onto the highway, Janice realized they were going to an area they had never been.

"Where exactly are we going?"

"Maryland, I think."

"Maryland? Where in Maryland?"

"Germantown, I think."

"That sounds like it's a place off the map."

"Don't worry. It's not like we're going to Baltimore or anything."

"What's there?"

"It's the place where the band practices. I'm just going to play a few sets for the guys to let them see what I can do."

Janice let her head fall back on the seat. Tonight was sure to be another one of Nick's long nights. She didn't know if she was up for it. Janice just finished a 12-hour shift, and she wanted to sleep. Nick leaned over and kissed her on the cheek.

"Hey, it won't be that bad."

"For you, maybe. For me? I'm tired."

"Once you hear me playing, that should wake you up."

"Yeah."

After driving up I-270 for what seemed like forever, the taxi took an exit and drove through an area that only had a few houses. Soon all the homes disappeared, and the cab bounced along a poorly paved road.

"Jesus," whispered Janice.

She could feel her teeth rattling in her head as the driver seemed to find every pothole in the road. Finally, the taxi turned into a parking lot next to a large warehouse.

"You sure you have the right place?" Janice asked Nick.

He removed the piece of paper he had in his jacket and confirmed the address.

"Yeah. This is the place."

The building was old and gray like it had once been a chemical plant of some kind. All the windows were smokey black to prevent visitors from looking inside. Aside from a few cars parked in the parking lot, there were no other signs of people in the area. Nick paid the taxi driver, and he and Janice got out. Nick banged on the door. Within a few seconds, they heard someone unlocking it.

"Who the fuck are you?" asked a girl with green hair.

Janice stared at the woman. The girl looked like she had been experimenting with every makeup product in her mother's collection.

"I'm Nick."

"Nick. What the fuck is a Nick?"

"I'm here to see Danny."

The girl turned around and yelled into the darkness.

"Hey D! Some nerdy-looking suck ass is here with his skanky bitch to see you!"

Janice got angry. She pushed Nick aside and got in the girl's face.

"Who the fuck do you think you..." Janice began.

But before she could finish her sentence, she was interrupted by a chubby guy with a shaved head.

"Hey, Nick! You made it! Come on in."

The girl frowned at Nick and Janice.

"You know these gross fucks?"

"Relax, Steph. They're cool. Grab a couple of beers from the fridge. Thanks."

The girl smacked her lips and stormed off.

"Wow. Your girl doesn't like us."

"Don't worry about her. Steph's cool once you get to know her. Come on in."

The couple followed Danny through a dark hallway into a large open room. Janice immediately started coughing. Cigarette and marijuana smoke was thick in the room.

"Virgin lungs, eh?" asked Danny as he smiled at Janice, trying to catch her breath. "Beer helps. We'll get that drink for you shortly."

Janice finished her bout of coughing and looked around. On the far end of the room were several electric guitars scattered on the floor. There were several microphones and a large drum set sitting in front of several small speakers. Sitting to their right on the mess was a group of people sitting on the dirty floor.

"Hey, guys! The motherfucking man is here!"

A thin guy with rainbow-colored hair stood up and looked at Nick.

"You can play, huh?" he asked.

"Hey Nick, this is Trick. He plays drums."

"Nick? Is that really his name?" asked Trick.

Danny ignored him and pointed to the other guys sprawled on the floor.

"Those other two dudes sitting over there are Jace and Turtle. They play bass and guitar."

"What's up, dude?" they both yelled.

"What's your instrument?" asked Trick.

"I play a little of everything."

"What's your favorite band?"

"I don't have one."

"Who's your favorite musician?"

"I like a lot, but I don't have a favorite."

Suddenly the group of people started giggling. Trick turned to Danny and laughed.

"He doesn't have a favorite band or artist? What kind of fucking poser did you bring us?"

"Hey, hey...let's not judge him until we hear him."

"Fine. Go over and play something."

The thin guy pointed to the group of instruments on the floor. Nick kissed Janice on the cheek.

"Go over to the wall and wait for me," Nick whispered.

After Janice went over and leaned against the wall, Nick walked over to the instruments and picked up the electric guitar from the floor. One of the girls walked behind him and turned on the power.

"What do you want to hear?"

"Beethoven!" yelled one of the men.

Once again, the group cracked up laughing.

Nick ran his fingers across the guitar strings and made several adjustments.

"Well? You going to play something or not?" asked one of the girls.

Without warning, Nick launched into playing one of his favorite songs. Janice watched in delight as the group grew silent. Janice had heard Nick play the same music when they were back home at his parent's house. It was a song he knew inside and out. Nick threw himself into his performance as a man focused. Little beads of sweat appeared on his forehead while he whirled around, kicking and swinging the guitar widely, wholly immersed in the music. Suddenly, one of the guys stood and went to the drums. Soon he began banging out a rhythm to accompany Nick's performance. Next, the other guys stood and went to grab their instruments. Soon the room filled with music.

The women that had once been half-dead on the floor stood up and started dancing wildly to the music the group was playing. Nick's playing intensified, and mouths fell open in awe of the music he was playing. The girl that had been so rude to the couple when they first arrived walked over to Janice and handed her a frosty mug of beer and an apologetic smile. Janice took the beer and rolled her eyes as if nullifying the girl's attempt at a half-assed apology.

Finally, Nick played the final note of the song and stopped playing.

"Holy fucking shit!" yelled Danny. "I had no fucking idea!"

The other band members were equally profuse in their congratulatory praise of Nick's performance.

"Dude! What will it take for you to join our band, naming my firstborn after you? You got it!" asked the drummer as he made his way around the instruments.

The two girls that had been thrashing their bodies to the music inched closer to Nick.

"You play good," said the blonde with big boobs.

Another girl with short hair made her attack from the rear.

"Where did you learn to play like that? You're awesome."

Janice's face turned red with anger. She was about to confront the girls when Nick laid down the guitar on the floor and walked over to her.

"Hey, I think we're going to go home now. We have a busy day tomorrow," Nick announced while hugging and kissing Janice.

"No way, dude. You have to give us an answer now. Don't leave us hanging like that," yelled Turtle, brushing his oily black hair from his pink eyes.

"Sorry, guys. Janice and I discuss things before we make a decision."

"Hey, that's cool. Janice, is it? Don't worry about Nick. He'll be in safe hands with this band. We're all like one big family here."

"One big family?" asked Janice as she looked at the two girls eyeing her boyfriend.

That's precisely what made her nervous.

Nick pulled Janice towards the door.

"I'll get back to you guys by noon tomorrow. Okay?"

Danny relented and began walking with Nick to the door.

"It's cool, bro. No worries. Just make sure you give us a buzz. You have my number, right?"

"Yeah, I have it."

"Cool."

Danny left Janice and Nick standing in the parking lot. After calling a taxi, Nick hugged his girlfriend.

"Well? How did I do?"

"You were awesome. I never doubted you."

"I was a ball of nerves in front of those guys. But I finally settled down."

"I didn't like those girls, though."

"I saw that. Why do you think I decided to leave? You have to control your temper, baby."

"Maybe. But those girls didn't give a damn about you until you started playing. After that, they became disgusting groupies."

"Well, don't worry about them. When I'm playing, I'm in the moment. I'm not thinking about girls."

Janice moved closer to Nick.

"You're not thinking of girls? Not even one?"

Nick kissed Janice and grabbed her butt.

"Maybe one."

"I'm taking it tonight."

"What? Oh, that."

"Why not? It's not every day that a girl gets to fuck her favorite Rockstar."

Nick laughed loudly.

"Who's the groupie now?"

"One night only."

Finally, the taxi arrived, and the couple climbed in.

18

Six Months Later

Sunday was Janice's only day off, so she slept in late. Nick and his band stayed up all night on Saturdays, and Janice wasn't surprised to wake up in bed alone. Since Nick had joined the group, he had given more time and energy to making his dream come true. Although the hours Nick spent away from home made Janice feel lonely, she tried to understand. Making dreams come true was a complicated process that required dedication. At least his band brought in money, and Nick didn't have to go out to find a job, so Janice was thankful for that much.

Janice rolled over and looked at the clock. It was 11 in the morning. As she lay in bed, loneliness crept over her. She missed Nick. There was no denying the fact that they'd started drifting apart. Nick used to make dinner for her once or twice a week. Now she was lucky if he was even there to share an ordered pizza with her. The sex had all but died. Aside from a kiss on the cheek when he got home, there was nothing. Playing in the band drained Nick of his energy, and all he did was sleep.

In addition to feeling lonely, Janice couldn't help feeling resentment building inside her. Janice and Nick spent no time on her dream of being a successful painter. Aside from a half-crinkled paint pad, Nick hadn't contributed anything to her goals. They hadn't gone to the museums as Nick had promised, and he always made up an excuse about why they couldn't go to any art exhibits in the city. It felt as though Nick only cared about what made him happy, and he expected Janice to stay at home being the supportive girlfriend. Finally, Janice swung her legs off the bed and sat up.

"Fuck this," Janice exclaimed.

It wasn't Nick's responsibility to make her dreams come true. It was hers. After showering and wolfing down a slice of leftover pizza, she dashed out of the apartment and caught a bus to the subway. As soon as Janice climbed on the train, she saw a girl sitting by the window that looked familiar. The girl stared back for a few seconds before she finally spoke.

"Janice?"

"Yes. I'm sorry, what's your name?"

"Wow. What a memory. It's me, Scarlett. The bartender?"

Suddenly Janice's memory came back to her.

"Scarlett! Now I remember! Sorry. My memory is shit when it comes to names. How have you been?"

Scarlett beckoned Janice to the open seat beside her.

"I've been okay. I stopped working at the club."

"You did? Why?"

"   My boyfriend got a new job at a law firm, and we decided I should go back to school."

"That's great! What are you studying?"

"Journalism. It's tedious, but I have no choice but to pay dues if I want to move up. What have you been up to?"

"Nothing much, really. I'm just trying to get set up in the city."

"You working?"

"Yeah. It's a little job at a bookstore for now, but it pays the bills until I find something better."

"Hey, you don't have to tell me. I did that crap for over two years."

"At least Nick found a job. He joined a band, and he's been making steady money."

"He plays? I didn't know that."

"Yeah. Lead guitar. Nick plays with the band that was performing at the club when we met."

"He plays with those guys? Your boyfriend must be good. They do a lot of club dates."

"So I'm finding out."

"You don't like it?"

"Not really. It's cutting into our time."

"Where are you going now?"

"I was going to check out a museum or two. We've been in the city for a while, and I haven't been to any of those places."

"Have you checked out the galleries over at Georgetown?"

"You mean the university?"

Scarlett burst out laughing.

"I forgot you're still new here. No. Georgetown is a part of DC that everyone goes to hang. I think they call it that because the university's close, but most people go there for shopping, galleries, and hanging out on the Potomac River."

"Really? It sounds complicated. I might get lost in a place like that."

"No, you wouldn't. I don't have anything to do all day. If you want, I could go with you. We could check out a few art galleries there."

"Really? That's so nice. Sure, I'd like that."

"Let's get off at the next stop and grab a cup of coffee. We'll take a taxi to Georgetown afterward."

"Nice."

As the women walked off the train, Janice started to feel better about her day. She was doing something without Nick, and it felt great.

19

What a Day

By the time Janice got off the bus at her apartment, the sun was setting, and she was exhausted. Her calves were on fire from all the walking she'd done with Scarlett. The two had spent hours in Georgetown, yet the time seemed to fly. Janice fell in love with Georgetown as soon as they arrived. Georgetown seemed like a small town hidden inside Washington, DC. There were quaint shops and unique restaurants that pulled her in like magnets. If her budget could afford it, she would've purchased something from each of the shops they visited. Instead, she settled on a set of red pumps and was grateful she'd left her debit card at home.

The art galleries in Georgetown were Janice's favorite. She never expected a place so off the beaten path to be so full of culture. Each gallery she visited seemed to pump her up more than the last. By the time the two had worn out enough shoe soles, Janice was so full of inspiration that she wanted to stop and start painting in the middle of the street. When Scarlett finally told her that she needed to get home, Janice was grateful. Although her legs hurt, she knew the first thing she'd do when she got home was to start painting the night away.

Janice entered her building and walked to her apartment. Just as she took her keys from her jeans, she heard a voice behind her.

"So, this is where you live."

Janice turned around to see her mother and stepfather approaching from the other end of the hall. She didn't know what to say. The only thing Janice could do was stare at the two of them with her mouth open. Finally, she spoke.

"What are you doing here?" asked Janice.

"What do you mean, what are we doing here? We're your parents. That's enough, isn't it?" replied her mother as she hugged her.

"Hey, Michael. How are you?"

Janice's stepdad looked angry. Instead of greeting Janice with a hug, he folded his arms and leaned against the wall.

"I'm fine. And how's the runaway?" Michael mumbled.

Janice's mother tapped her husband's arm.

"Michael, we promised we wouldn't fight. Remember?"

Janice's mother turned back to her.

"Well, aren't you going to invite us in?"

Janice looked reluctantly at her stepfather before finally relenting. She stuck her key in the door and unlocked it.

"This is just a starting place for us. Just something small until we can get on our feet."

Janice's parents walked in. After standing in the middle of the floor for a few moments, Janice's mother finally spoke.

"Well, it's...cute."

Janice's stepfather was less political in his assessment of the studio apartment.

"This place looks like shit. Is this the reason you ran away? To share closet space with that jerk?"

Janice's mother's eyes widened.

"Michael! Stop!"

"Stop what? You expect me to be okay with this? She's caused us all this stress, and for what? For this?"

Janice's face was red with anger.

"We're chasing our dreams, Michael! But I wouldn't expect you to understand that."

"You see, Shannon. This is your bullshit. All this validating of her emotions for all these years finally blew up in your face."

"Nothing's blown up, Michael. I'm happy! I'm doing what is best for me."

"So you expect me to believe you're okay with living in this shit hole?"

"It's better than living in a small town with a shitty job and a husband that beats me!"

Suddenly the room grew quiet. Michael glared at Janice.

"You need to watch your goddamned mouth!"

"No! You're in my house! You need to watch *your* mouth!"

Michael slapped Janice, and she fell onto the bed. Shannon ran to her daughter and grabbed her.

"Michael! What the hell is wrong with you?"

"And it's more where that came from. We've been too nice to this kid. Maybe that's what she's needed all along."

"She's a young woman! You don't…"

"You watch your goddamned mouth! I'm not taking any shit from anyone here. Get her to pack her shit, and we're leaving in fifteen minutes!"

Janice pushed her mother aside and stood up.

"I'm not going anywhere. You are!"

"What?"

"Who do you think you are? Do you think you can come in and hit me? This is my house. Mine!"

Michael made a fist and took a step towards Janice.

"What are you going to do? Punch me? Go ahead! But I'm not going anywhere!"

"You'll go where I tell you to go!"

"Who the hell do you think you are? You come here with your chest all stuck out like you run the world. You're not even my fucking dad! How dare you put your hands on me!"

Janice walked to her front door, unlocked it, and held it open.

"You have exactly one minute to move through that door. After that, I'm calling the police to report you for assault."

Shannon jumped to her feet.

"Janice, stop! You're taking things too far! We only came here to..."

"Oh please, mom! Save the drama. I know the reason you came here, and it's not because you're concerned. This visit is all about Michael's control and ego. I'm tired of pretending he likes me, and I like him. The truth is I hate his fucking guts. Any man that puts his hands on my mother is a piece of shit! I'm not you, mom. I won't tolerate him putting his hands on me!"

Shannon's eyes widened.

"What?"

"That's right. I'm not you! I could never stay with a man that beats me."

Michael began shaking with anger.

"You don't know what the fuck you're talking about!"

Janice pushed the door open wider.

"What? Are you still here? I thought I told you to get out!"

Janice reached into her pocket and pulled out her cell phone. She dialed the nine and the one and then held the phone up for her father to see it.

"Don't test me, Michael. I will call the police and have your ass locked up."

Michael raised his fist to hit Janice when her mother ran and stood in front of her daughter.

"Just go to the car, Michael. We'll be out in a few minutes, okay? Let me handle this."

"She's lost her fucking mind if she thinks she can talk to me like that."

"Go, baby. We'll be out in a few minutes."

Reluctantly, Michael glared at Janice before finally walking out of the apartment.

"Janice, what the hell has gotten into you?"

"What do you think, mom? He hit me!"

"I know, but he's your dad and…"

"Stop saying that! Michael is not my fucking dad! Just because you two raised me, it doesn't give him the right to put his hands on me!"

"You're right. You're right. But…"

"I'm in the city trying to make a life for myself. I thought you two would be proud of me!"

Suddenly Shannon became angry.

"Are you serious, Janice? Really?"

"Yes!"

"Proud of you? How? By celebrating the fact that you ran away to be with some asshole boyfriend that we caught having sex with you in our home? Get real!"

"You see! You're always judging me!"

"You're goddamned right we are! If you look up the word *parent* in the dictionary, you'd see the word *judge* right beside it!"

Janice burst into tears. She rubbed the side of her face and flopped down on the bed.

"What do you want from me?"

"We're here because we want to understand."

"No, you don't. You're here because you want me to go home."

"Yeah…that too. But…"

"I'm not going home, okay?"

"I'm being nice right now. I could say a lot of things that you don't want to hear."

"What? Getting slapped by Michael wasn't enough? Go ahead, mom. Shoot your best shot!"

"You threatening to call the police on your stepdad was going too far."

"I was only going to do something you should've done years ago."

Shannon turned away from Janice as tears filled her eyes. Quietly, she walked to the door. She opened it and turned to face her daughter.

"You want to make us out to be the demons here. I get it. Youth rules the world. It's like that for everyone when they're young. But think about this. At any moment, your stepfather and I could've called the police and had your boyfriend arrested for statutory rape and kidnapping."

Janice's mouth dropped open.

"That's right. We found out when that boy's parents came to our house. Did we do that? No."

"You wouldn't hurt us like that."

"No, you're wrong! We *could've* and probably *should've*, but *didn't*!"

"Why not?"

"Flexibility and common sense are how we chose to handle your situation. Teenagers don't know about being flexible, and they damn sure don't know about common sense. But responsible parents know what those words mean. In time, you'll figure out what those words mean too. Maybe then you'll come to understand how much disrespect you've shown us and how grateful you should be that we didn't call the cops on the two of you."

"We're not criminals."

"Neither are we. So while you're out here running around this big city, remember that you're able to do so at the generosity of a so-called abusive man that raised you and could've called the cops on Nick whenever he felt like being a dick about it."

Shannon walked out of the door and closed it behind her. Terrified and shaken, Janice fell on the bed, buried her face in her pillow, and started sobbing. Her perfect day turned out to be one that she wanted to forget. After a few minutes of emptying her pain into the pillow, Janice got up, grabbed her keys, and left the apartment. She had to tell Nick about the confrontation she'd just had with her parents.

20

Seeking Comfort Through Pain

When the cab pulled up to the front of the old building, Janice seemed confused. There were a lot of cars in the parking lot. She'd never seen the place have more than four vehicles when she visited. She paid the driver and climbed out of the car. Just as Janice exited the vehicle, two women burst out of the building, doubled over in laughter. One was a tall brunet, and the other was a short chubby redhead. They were wearing short skirts, and both were drunk.

"Fucking awesome!" one of the women yelled. "How much did you drink?"

"Enough! I'm fucking blitzed!" the other woman replied.

The two women walked up to Janice and continued laughing.

"Who the fuck are you here to see?" asked one of the girls, her breasts spilling out of her loosely fit shirt.

Janice backed away from the pair. Their breath smelled like vomit and gin. Suddenly her friend jumped into the conversation.

"No way, bitch. You're not going to get laid looking like that. Get back in your cab and go somewhere else."

The two women started cracking up again.

"Did you do your makeup, or did you just slam your face in some mud?"

Janice angrily walked between the two women, almost knocking them to the ground.

"Hey, bitch! Watch where you're going!" Janice heard one girl say.

But by then, she'd already entered the building.

Once Janice was inside the building, she moved through the poorly lit room as if she been there a million times. Janice ignored the people standing around smoking cigarettes and pushed past the people that seemed to question if she was in the wrong place. She saw a couple of the band members flirting with girls in the corner of the room and ducked in the shadows to avoid them. Janice didn't want the world to know about her crying. When she finally made it to the area where the band practiced, she expected to see most of the band members rehearsing. Instead, what Janice saw was a large congregation of people sipping beers and standing around laughing. After a few minutes, she spotted a familiar face she felt comfortable engaging. It was Danny.

"Hey! Danny!" Janice yelled.

The chubby guy squinted to see who had called him. After a while, he finally spoke.

"Oh, hey. How's it going?"

"I'm trying to find Nick. Is he here?"

"Yeah, he's here somewhere. Wait a sec. I'll see if I can find him for you."

Danny walked away quickly through the crowd of people with Janice in tow. He opened the door to a dark hallway and yelled.

"Nick! Hey Nick!"

Janice reached the door and pushed it open. Through the poorly lit hallway, she saw Nick sitting on the floor. A blonde girl was kissing him while another girl's head moved up and down on his lap.

"Nick!" Danny yelled, trying to shield Janice from what was going on.

"What the fuck is it?" asked Nick, pushing the girl aside. Suddenly his eyes fell on Janice's face, and he jumped up, his pants falling around his ankles.

"Janice! Baby! It's not what..."

But he was only talking to the three other people in the hallway. Janice had taken one look at what her boyfriend was doing and ran out of the room.

21

Told You So

As Janice pushed through the crowd of people, she could feel her heartbeat ringing in her ears. The image of what she'd just witnessed was so jarring that she felt drunk, dizzy from the painful images her eyes consumed. Janice didn't hear Danny walking behind her, offering to call her a taxi. Nor did she hear the numerous people staring at her as she made her way to the door. The only thing she could truly feel were the eyes of shame from every person in the building. They were all in on Nick's secret. They had to be. Nick's blatant disregard for privacy during his sexual escapades showed experience. What Janice witnessed wasn't the first time Nick had sex in public with strangers. Janice was sure of it. It was just the first incident Janice saw.

As soon as Janice opened the door, she burst into tears. She started sprinting across the parking lot and up the dark street. Janice didn't know where she was going, but she wanted to get as far away from that place as she could. Images of Nick having sex kept flashing in her mind like bursts of poison. How could he be so evil? How could he betray her like that? Her mind started thinking about all the things they did together in bed. Soon Janice felt like vomiting. Maybe Nick had sex with those girls before coming home to her.

When Janice finally stopped crying, she was miles away from the building. There were no houses around, only dark trees that made her sadness even more challenging to endure. She pulled out her cell phone and called a taxi. She didn't know where she was, but Janice told the dispatcher the area she had previously been. After she hung up, she flopped down on the edge of the road and waited.

While she sat on the ground, Janice thought about all the ways her family had been right about Nick. The two of them having sex in her parent's house was the ultimate sign of selfishness on both their part, but now, considering Nick's infidelity, her boyfriend's selfishness stuck out like a sore thumb. Janice cursed herself for being so blind.

"I could be driving back home with mom and Michael right now," she yelled into the darkness.

Suddenly, the images of her boyfriend having sex clouded Janice's thoughts. Angrily, she burst into a fresh bout of crying. Janice couldn't believe she'd risked it all to move to the city with Nick. She'd told her mom how different Nick was. Now her words to her mom sounded like self-righteous crap. What would her parents say if she told them about what happened? For a moment, Janice fantasized about getting revenge.

"If I called Michael, he'd be here tomorrow to kick Nick's ass," Janice whispered.

Or maybe she could tell her parents to go to the police and push them to file statutory rape charges.

Janice hugged her knees and lowered her head. She could do none of those things because she still loved Nick. And no matter what he'd done, Janice didn't want to see him hurt. Not by anything she'd done.

Finally, a set of headlights appeared from far away. Janice stood up, turned on her cellphone's flashlight, and waved it back and forth. The vehicle slowed and stopped in front of her.

"Janice?" the driver asked. Janice opened the door and climbed in.

"That's me."

"Where are you going tonight?"

"Just take me to the closest hotel. A decent one if you don't mind."

"Will do."

Janice laid her head against the window and watched the car move through the darkness. There was no way she was going back to the apartment. Nick was bound to show up there with his drama, and Janice didn't have the energy to relive that nightmare. She just wanted to sleep.

22 |

Misery

Janice was supposed to work the next day, but she called out sick. Although it was her first time using that excuse to avoid work, it felt appropriate as she battled the previous night's reality. Janice got up and ordered breakfast from room service, but as soon as the hotel delivered the food, Janice threw it on the table, disgusted at the thought of eating. She climbed in bed for four more hours, unable and unwilling to gather enough energy to shower. As Janice laid in bed, she heard the buzz of her phone vibrating on the nightstand.

"Fuck you, asshole," Janice barked as she silenced the ringer.

It was surely Nick calling to see where she was. The mere thought of even hearing his voice made her want to vomit. After a few more minutes of listening to Nick blow up her cellphone, Janice turned on the television and watched a few hours of news. There was a story about a string of murders that happened the previous night.

"I died last night too," she mumbled to the television. At that moment, a knock came at the door.

"Housekeeping," a woman yelled from the hallway.

"No, not today. I'm fine," Janice replied.

She didn't feel like dealing with anyone. Wallowing in grief was the only activity she wanted to do.

At 4 pm, her cell phone rang again. This time Janice picked up the phone and looked at the number. It was Scarlett.

"Hello?" Janice asked.

"Wow. Someone sounds like she had a rough night," replied Scarlett.

"Like you wouldn't believe."

"Are you up for dinner?"

"I'm kind of out of it."

"Oh, come on. There's this new Italian restaurant I've been dying to visit."

"Well..."

"Look. Greg is traveling and won't be back until tomorrow morning. It'll be fun to just have dinner in the city. Just us girls."

Janice sat up in bed and looked at her watch. Nick would probably be out of the apartment, and she could run home to change her clothing. Besides, she was starving.

"Okay. You twisted my arm. I'm game."

"Great! I'll give you a couple of hours to get yourself together. You can meet me at the Metro Station, and we can catch the train to the restaurant."

"Sure. I'll see you in a couple of hours."

You Cannot Run Forever

Janice unlocked her apartment door and walked inside. There was a pair of Nick's jeans sitting at the foot of the bed, and she kicked them to the other side of the room.

"Fucking idiot," she mumbled.

Just as the jeans hit the wall, Nick opened the bathroom door and walked out.

"Where have you been?"

"Go to hell."

Janice walked to the closet and pulled down her suitcase.

"What is that for?"

"What do you think? I'm leaving."

"Just like that? You're not going to listen to anything I have to say?"

"What? You can't be serious. What could you possibly say to explain that bitch's tongue down your throat? How could you explain the nasty slut giving you a blowjob?"

"I wasn't thinking straight. Danny gave me some pills, and I…"

"Oh, now it's the *I was drugged* excuse. Fuck you!"

"Well, I was!"

"Look! I want you to get the fuck out of this apartment! Now!"

"You don't mean that."

"I do! I don't trust you anymore! You're a sick fucking liar! I should've let my stepdad blow your head off!"

"You don't mean that."

"Don't tell me what I mean and what I don't! I do mean it! What kind of sick person would do something so horrible? Now I have to get tested for venereal diseases, and God knows what else!"

"It only happened once."

"What kind of fool do you think I am? It only takes one time to get HIV, you dumb idiot!"

"I'll get tested. Is that what you want?"

"No! I want you out of this apartment!"

"I'm not going anywhere!"

Janice was shaking with anger and crying furiously.

"Fine! If you're not going, then I am!"

Janice tossed clean and dirty clothes into her luggage and zipped it up.

"Hey! What are you doing?" yelled Nick.

He ran to Janice and snatched the suitcase out of her hands.

"You're not going anywhere!"

"Stop, Nick! Get away from me! The sight of you makes me want to throw up! I hate you!"

"You don't mean that. You're just upset."

"I do mean it! Everything you told me was a lie! All of those words about how you would never hurt me were all bullshit!"

Nick tried to hug Janice, and she smacked him in the face. She immediately ran into the bathroom and locked the door. Nick ran to the door and tried to open it.

"Baby. Could you please open the door so we can talk about this?"

"Just go, Nick!"

Nick grabbed Janice's luggage and stuffed it back into the closet.

"I'm not going anywhere until you talk to me. It was an accident."

Janice turned on the shower and took her clothes off. As Nick begged and pleaded for her to open the door, she climbed into the shower. Janice didn't have time to hear Nick's nonsense. She needed to get out of the apartment before she strangled him.

Once she finished showering, Janice brushed her teeth and blow-dried her hair. She put her ear close to the door to see if Nick was still there. She could hear the television, but her boyfriend had stopped trying to talk to her through the door. Janice wrapped herself in a towel and walked out.

Nick was sitting on the edge of the bed watching television. He nervously stood and turned it off before turning to face Janice.

"You still want me to go?"

Janice walked to the closet and pulled some clothes out of her suitcase. Without looking in his direction, she responded to Nick's question.

"I think it would be best for a few days. I need time to get my head together."

Nick was quiet for a few seconds, and then he spoke.

"I think we should tackle this problem head-on. Time away from one another could make everything worse. Don't you think?"

"It's what I need, Nick. I'm too angry to talk about anything right now. Just give me a few days to get my head together."

Nick sighed and grabbed his jacket.

"We're doing a couple of club dates, so I'll be returning in two days. Is that enough time?"

Janice didn't answer. She climbed into her clothes and went to the mirror to put on her makeup. Nick stood in the center of the floor, watching Janice apply her foundation. Janice glanced at him through the mirror and quickly looked away. Nick had a pathetic look on his face like a sad puppy who'd lost his favorite toy. Still, Janice felt no remorse for her boyfriend. She wanted him gone.

Finally, Nick opened the door and prepared to leave.

"I'll call you from the road," he murmured, waiting for a response from Janice. She gave him nothing and applied her lipstick as if he wasn't even in the room.

Deflated, Nick walked out.

A Night Without Men

Dinner with Scarlett lifted Janice's spirits immensely. After pouring her heart out about her relationship, Janice was on the edge of bursting into tears when the funniest thing happened. A waiter passed their table carrying a large cake while all the waiters swarmed from different parts of the room to sing Happy Birthday. As the waiter placed the cake on the table for the birthday kid to blow out his candles, the kid grabbed a handful of cake and threw it at his little brother. The child ducked, and the cake hit an elderly man in his face. The man was so surprised that he opened his mouth to complain, and his dentures fell into his glass of wine. All the restaurant patrons saw the incident, and everyone burst into laughter – including Scarlett and Janice. After witnessing such a hilarious episode, Janice could barely take a bite of food without looking at the old man's table and bursting into laughter.

After dinner, they went back to Scarlett's apartment to watch tv and talk. Janice was still too shaken at the possibility that Nick, choosing to shirk his responsibilities, would be at the apartment looking for round two.

Scarlett stayed in Adams Morgan, the lively part of DC that all the college students chose to visit to get wasted. Scarlett and her boyfriend rented a small brownstone on a side street, away from the bars and restaurants.

"Your home is nice," said Janice as she walked in.

"It'll do. Rent's so high we get nosebleeds, but it's close to everything and within walking distance to nothing. It's okay. Have a seat."

Janice looked around the house in amazement. There were beautiful vases and photos of their families all around the room. The carpet on the floor was so lush it made Janice want to take off her shoes.

"How long have you guys been here?"

"About eight months."

"This place is awesome."

"It's not as nice as it seems. Sometimes we can hear the noise from the street, and we can't sleep. And the parking? Gosh! I've got a metal boot on my car three times since we've been here."

"A metal boot?"

"Yeah. It's this big metal lock the city places on one of the wheels of your car for failing to pay parking tickets. It's just a revenue scam."

"Oh."

Scarlett poked her head out from the kitchen and held up a bottle of wine.

"Want some?"

"What? Wine? I'd better not. It'll probably have me flooding your house with tears."

Scarlett placed the wine on the counter.

"You know what? I have just the thing to help you out."

Scarlett walked upstairs. Seconds later, she came back holding a brown wooden box and a pipe.

"What's that?"

"Just what we need to mellow you out. Don't worry. It's not too strong. But it takes the edge off."

"Is that...weed?"

"Yep."

Janice held up her hands in protest.

"No, no. I couldn't. I've never done it before."

"Really? You don't know what you're missing."

Scarlett sat on the sofa beside Janice and opened the box. Inside was a plastic bag filled with clumps of a strange plant.

"So, what did you catch Nick doing?" asked Scarlett as she stuffed the strong-smelling plant into the pipe.

"Having sex with two girls."

"Really?"

"Yeah. It was horrible."

"What did he say? Did he give you a lame ass excuse?"

"Of course. Nick told me he was drugged and didn't know what he was doing."

"Piece of shit. You didn't buy that crap, did you?"

"Hell no. Just because we're from the South, it doesn't mean I'm Country-Dumb. How are you not going to know when someone's blowing you?"

Scarlett lifted a crystal gas lighter from underneath the table and put the pipe to her lips.

"You don't mind, do you?"

"It's your house."

"Cool. So, what are you going to do?"

"I don't know. What do you think I should do?"

Scarlett took a deep drag on the pipe and held it in for a few moments before exhaling and speaking.

"No way, girl."

"What?"

"Never ask a friend for advice about your man."

"Why not?"

"Because if it blows up in your face, the friend gets the blame for giving bad advice. It's a lose-lose situation."

"Well, I think I should leave. That image of Nick and those two girls are on the inside of my eyelids like graffiti. How can I ever look at him the same way?"

Scarlett took another deep drag on the pipe and exhaled.

"Greg cheated on me."

"He did?"

"Yeah. Some dumb ass bimbo at his office."

"How did you find out?"

"I went to his office unannounced before he was leaving, and I saw him kiss her goodbye."

"Shit!"

"Oh yeah, girl. Talk about drama? I threw all his shit out on the street and changed the locks. I was nuts."

"Really?"

"Yep."

"How did the two of you resolve it?"

"I fucked one of his friends."

"What the..."

"Oh, I didn't do it as revenge. It happened before I found out Greg was sleeping with the girl at his job. One time Greg went out of town when I was working at the club. I was drunk, and the guy was drunk. It just happened. I didn't know until I went into Greg's office that he worked with the guy. While I was so busy judging Greg, I'd forgotten that I cheated on him first."

"And he knew?"

"Yep. Greg said he never said anything about it because he didn't know how to bring up the subject. But I think he just wanted to use it as an excuse to fuck around on me."

"Deep. It sounds like you two had major trust issues."

"Who doesn't? It just gets to the point where you have to be honest with one another. I would always catch Greg looking at other women and never thought anything of it. I thought it was just something that all men did, you know? Meanwhile, I would steal looks at the men in the club and pretend I was immune to being anything other than the perfect girlfriend. But the truth is, we're all imperfect. Everyone makes mistakes."

"Maybe. But you didn't see what I saw. Can you imagine seeing that girl in your boyfriend's office giving your man a blowjob?"

"No, because I'd cut his dick off."

The two women burst into laughter. Once again, Scarlett held the pipe out for Janice to take it.

"Aw, what the hell," she said as she took the pipe and lifted it to her lips.

"You're a newbie, so you'd better take a small puff."

Janice took a puff and held it in her mouth.

"Now breath it into your lungs like you're holding your breath in a swimming pool. But don't breathe out. Hold it in for as long as you can."

Janice held her breath for about three seconds before coughing.

"Jesus. How do you do that stuff?" she asked while passing the pipe back to Scarlett.

"Aw, shut up. You're just green, that's all."

Janice tasted the pungent odor in her mouth and sat back on the sofa. Smoking wasn't as bad as she'd thought it would be. Calmly, Janice waited until Scarlett took another drag and then took the pipe from her. This time she pulled more of the smoke from the pipe and held it in her lungs.

"Look at the expert. Pretty soon, you're going to be showing me how to do tricks," joked Scarlett.

Suddenly it hit her.

A warm sensation crawled up from her toes and settled inside her cheeks. Janice's eyes felt sleepy, and everything seemed to move. Slowly, Janice began to smile and then suddenly started laughing hysterically. Scarlett took another drag on the pipe and laughed at Janice.

"Yep. You're feeling it now, aren't you?"

Janice leaned over on the arm of the chair and tried to touch the floor.

"This is fucking awesome!" she exclaimed, her words tumbling from her mouth in slow motion.

"Yeah, I knew you'd like it. You're not thinking about Nick now, are you?"

"Nick? Who the fuck is that? Fuck that asshole."

Scarlett burst into laughter.

"That's my girl! No crying over here."

"I don't need him. Do you know I pay for almost all of our expenses?"

"Really?"

"Yeah. Nick spent almost all his money on a guitar. We wouldn't have a studio if I didn't bite the bullet and get that job at the bookstore."

"My God! Why are you with that prick? He's such a loser!"

"And he has the nerve to let some skank suck his shriveled-up pecker!"

"Pecker? Now that's a word I haven't heard for years and years!"

Janice took another drag on the pipe and held her breath before continuing to speak.

"You know what? He's not even good in bed."

"Get out!"

"He can't even give me ten good strokes without turning to mush."

Once again, Scarlett burst out laughing. After she caught her breath, she looked around the room.

"I'm fucking hungry. You?" Scarlett asked Janice.

"I could eat. What do you have in the kitchen?"

"I've got a box of leftover pizza from last night."

"Sounds good to me."

Scarlett went to the kitchen and pulled the box of pizza out of the refrigerator.

"You know," Scarlett yelled. "You should just let that motherfucker twist in the breeze. Give him a week or two to think about the pain he put you through. That'll teach him a lesson he'll never forget."

Scarlett grabbed the bottle of wine from the counter and walked back into the living room.

"Yeah. Just let that son of a…"

She froze in her tracks. Janice was lying on the couch, sound asleep. Scarlett went to her closet and retrieved a blanket, and covered Janice with it. She took the pizza out of the oven, dimmed the lights, and went upstairs to her bedroom.

25

What Love is Worth

Janice woke up in a slight panic. As she looked around the dark living room, she forgot where she was. But after a few minutes, her memory returned to her, and Janice realized she was still at Scarlett's house. Janice had an awful taste in her mouth – like someone had poured glue into it.

"Jesus. Disgusting," Janice whispered.

She'd heard weed smokers at her high school complain about *Cotton Mouth*, but she'd never experienced it before. The thick saliva made her tongue almost stick to the roof of her mouth. Although it was dark, Janice could feel small clumps of spit gathering in the corners of her mouth. She quickly wiped her mouth with the sleeve of her shirt.

Janice looked at the loveseat adjacent to the sofa to see if Scarlett had fallen asleep there, but it was empty. After realizing Scarlett probably went upstairs, Janice folded her blanket and placed it neatly on the sofa. She spotted a small desk in the corner of the room and retrieved a pen and piece of paper from it. She scribbled a thank you note for Scarlett and placed it on the living room table. Quietly, Janice opened the front door of the house and inched out.

As Janice rode the train home, she began to think about Nick. Who was with her boyfriend? What was he doing? Janice's mind could only imagine the worst. In her mind, her boyfriend was with the same set of girls, doing the same disgusting thing. Although her common sense told her that Nick was fucking whoever he wanted, Janice's mind held on to the possibility that he was telling the truth. What if his friends did take advantage of him? Wasn't Nick the victim as much as she was?

"No. Nick's guilty," Janice whispered.

She remembered how sober Nick had gotten when he'd seen her standing in the doorway. He'd even had the sense of mind to pull his pants up. People who are drugged wouldn't be able to do that.

By the time Janice got on the bus for her final ride to the apartment, she was deep in her hatred of Nick. How could he be so careless? How could Nick claim to love her if he could throw it all away so easily? Janice pulled out her cell phone and flipped to her calendar. She set herself a reminder to call her gynecologist to have herself checked out. Next, she flipped one month ahead and placed a note on October 1st. On that date, she typed the following words:

Leave Nick

26

Motherly Advice

When Janice finally arrived at her apartment, it was 9 am. She felt a hunger deep in her stomach that she'd never felt before.

"The munchies," Janice said while rifling through the refrigerator, looking for anything edible. After cutting herself a big slice of cheddar cheese, she whipped up four eggs and made herself a gigantic cheese and tomato omelet. After wolfing it down, Janice cleaned the apartment and showered. When she finished, she went to work at the bookstore. The store was so busy that no one had time even to question her absence. Janice wasn't on the schedule to work, but the supervisor begged her to stay. Janice didn't mind. After her extended stay in the hotel, she needed the money. Plus, if Janice stayed at home, she'd only be fantasizing about a million ways she'd cut Nick's dick off. Working was a way to take her mind off her misery.

By the time Janice arrived home from work, she was thoroughly exhausted. She pulled off her clothes and fell on the bed. Although Janice wanted to sleep, she couldn't. After a few moments of thinking, Janice picked up her cell phone and dialed her mother.

"Hello?"

"Mom? It's me."

"Oh. Is everything okay?"

"Yeah. Everything's fine."

There was a moment of silence before Janice's mother spoke again.

"Okay, let's have it."

"What?"

"I know my daughter. What's bothering you?"

"Nothing."

There was another uncomfortable pause before Janice spoke.

"It's Nick."

"What happened?"

"I want to tell you, mom, but you have to promise to keep quiet about this."

"I will promise no such thing."

"Why?"

"Because if it's something horrible, I can't hide something like that from Michael."

"It's not life or death, mom."

"Fine. Then let's have it."

Janice took a deep breath and spoke.

"Nick cheated on me."

Janice's mother remained silent.

"Aren't you going to say anything?"

"What do you expect me to say?"

"I don't know. Something? Anything? I told you so, or come home?"

"Nope. I'm not going to feed you a lot of foolishness like that. You're an adult now, and you need to start handling your life as a woman should."

"You're my mom."

"And I'll always be your mom. The only thing I can say to you is this. The difference between being a starry-eyed daughter and a responsible adult is as wide as the Grand Canyon. Nobody wants to tell the truth about that gulf, and so the road is littered with skin from peeled knees and falls that people make to get to the other side. I had to make that trip and got hurt along the way. So did Michael. Now it's your turn."

"It's not that I want you to decide for me. I just wanted to talk to somcone about it."

The two women were quiet for a few moments.

"Janice."

"Yes, mom?"

"The heart of a man is dark. There are truths he'll tell his friends that he'll never admit to you. The way most of us women discover the depths of that darkness is when that darkness tries to eat us."

"I thought Nick was different, mom. Before we came to the city, we didn't have any secrets. I assumed Nick and I shared everything."

"You don't, and you never will."

"Wow, mom. You sound bitter."

"Is that what you think it is? Bitterness? Your real father skated out on me when I was pregnant with his child. If I were going to be bitter, that would've been the thing that pushed me there. But I wasn't because I understood."

"I know, but you're implying every man is bad."

"Well...live a little on this earth and get the answers for yourself."

"Mom. Can I ask you a question?"

"I couldn't stop you if I wanted to."

"Why don't you ever say his name?"

"Who?"

"My father. I notice you never speak his name."

"I don't know. I don't think it's intentional. Alex is like a ghost in my life. I can barely remember what he looks like."

"Why do you keep trying to replace him with Michael?"

Janice's mother paused before responding.

"I confess. I do that intentionally."

"Why? Don't you think it's important for me to know who my father is? Who he was?"

"Your stepdad Michael is a man living in reality. He pays bills, takes care of you when you're sick, and puts food on the table. Your father, Alex, was a teenager living in a dream. He pumped my head full of romantic notions of how our lives would be. When that boy spoke to me, I tell you, clouds parted, and sweet sunshine warmed my face. I believed what he told me about being together forever. But when push came to shove, all of those sweet words turned to dog shit. You can't make a boy into a man overnight. Reality made him shit his pants, and he ran away. And as I lay in my mother's trailer singing to you at night, I had to accept the fact that Alex lied to me. And I guess the reason I never say his name is because I wanted you to get a clear idea of the difference between what's real and what's not."

Janice felt her heartbreaking. Hearing the truth from her mother about her real father was one of the most crushing things she'd ever heard in her life. Janice felt the pain and regret in her mother's words. It was something she'd never heard before – or maybe something she never wanted to hear.

"So what do I do about Nick?"

"Decide for yourself what you can tolerate and what you can't. Like it or not, there's a price for everything."

"What am I supposed to do? Settle for abuse? Infidelity?"

"Nobody told you that you have to settle for anything. But it does all boil down to how much you love yourself. Truth be told, none of us *needs* anyone. Last I checked, porn is a billion-dollar business. You can always satisfy yourself without a man."

Janice burst into laughter.

"Mom!"

"It's true. Half the men can't do the right things in the bedroom anyway."

Janice was surprised by her mother's frank conversation. She didn't sound like her mother at all.

"Well, you do have a point," Janice responded, unsure of how much she should push such a subject with her mother.

"But for those of us that understand life, I mean truly understand it. There's a price to pay for love. And no one can put that shit on layaway."

"You're funny, mom."

"So figure it out, Janice. If Nick's worth it, keep him. If not, fuck him. Just decide. No one can decide for you."

"Okay. I'm going to bed now. Thanks for talking to me, mom."

"I'm here when you need me. Always. Goodnight."

Janice ended her phone call and tucked herself in her warm blanket. Maybe things weren't completely hopeless with her and Nick. She just needed to decide if their relationship was worth the work.

27

One Month Later

Janice was sleeping when she felt something cold on the back of her neck. She recognized the feeling. It was Nick rubbing his cold nose up and down the nape of her neck, asking for morning sex in his cute way. Usually, Janice would roll over and give him everything he wanted. Sex in the morning was her favorite. It was nasty, smelly, and moist – all the elements she loved about being intimate. But ever since Nick cheated on her, they stopped making love.

Nick tried his best to push past the hesitation and rejection, but Janice shot him down every time. All she could think of was that vision of what he'd done with the other women. She just wasn't ready. This morning was no different. She turned over to face him and broke into a fit of coughing, pushing horrendous morning breath and a mist of spit into his face. When Janice finished coughing and opened her eyes, the look of disgust on Nick's face told her that her tactic had been successful in pushing him away. Eventually, she spoke.

"Did I get you? I'm sorry," Janice said as she wiped Nick's face.

He turned away from Janice and got up to go to the bathroom. When he came out, Janice pretended she was asleep and was facing the opposite direction.

"How much longer are we going to go through this?" Nick asked.

Janice turned to face him and opened her eyes.

"What are we talking about?" she asked, pretending to wipe the sleep from her eyes.

"You know."

"If I knew, Nick, I wouldn't ask."

"We don't make love anymore."

"Well, I think you can answer that one for yourself. What do you think infidelity brings, a desire to fuck?"

"You can't keep punishing me for that. It's not fair."

Janice stood and went into the bathroom. After peeing, she came back out and faced Nick.

"I'm just not ready for that type of intimacy right now. I'm not saying that it's going to be like this forever. Just let me find my way back to you on my own."

"And in the meantime, what do you expect me to do? Walk around with an erection 24/7?"

"Nick. Stop."

"Stop what? You're not the one getting spit on first thing in the morning to avoid making love."

"What do you want from me? I just can't erase what I saw!"

"You don't have to let it dominate you either! I told you I didn't know what was going on!"

"So what! That doesn't make what happened any different in my eyes. All I see is those two bitches fucking you!"

Nick walked to the refrigerator and pulled out a cold beer.

"You see? This is how cheating starts."

"What? Are you fucking kidding me?"

"A man comes home and tries to be faithful. But no. Women always have to find ways to be unappreciative."

"You have got to be kidding me! This is how cheating starts?! We fucked all the time, and you still cheated on me! Now you want to complain because there are consequences for your actions? Nobody told you to let that girl blow you!"

"Maybe she wouldn't have had to blow me if..."

Janice's eyes widened, and she walked over to stand in front of Nick.

"Go ahead. Finish it!"

"Leave me the fuck alone."

"No. You started this. Maybe she wouldn't have had to blow you if what?"

"Nothing. This is going nowhere."

"I know what you were going to say. *Maybe she wouldn't have had to blow you if I gave you head more often?* Or maybe you were going to say: *maybe she wouldn't have had to blow you if I knew how to fuck you better.* Right?"

"I don't want to fight."

"You piece of shit! I'm supposed to be the woman you love and respect! I'm not a sex toy! I'm not your fucking pornstar!"

"Well, we both know *that* don't we?"

Janice swung at Nick's face with her fist and missed. He grabbed her arm and pushed her against the stove, knocking the metal kettle to the floor.

"Drama queen!"

Janice was crying and almost screaming at the top of her lungs.

"How could you say such things to me? I thought you loved and respected me."

"You started the whole fucking thing!"

"Fuck you, Nick!"

"You're not the only one that has needs. I have needs too! And if you won't satisfy them, someone else will!"

Janice ripped off her bra and threw it at Nick.

"Is this what you want? Come on, take it! That's all I am to you is a fucking piece of meat. Go ahead! Take it!"

Janice stepped out of her panties and threw them at her boyfriend.

"Come on! Fuck me! This is what you want, isn't it? Forget Janice, The Woman. You want Janice, The Nasty Slut, right?"

Nick stormed to the closet and pulled out his luggage.

"This isn't working. Maybe we do need to break up!"

"After what you said, you're goddamned right. Fuck you!"

"Tomorrow, when you're here all alone, you'll regret this."

"I'm here all alone anyway! What's the difference?"

"We could've been happy if you let the past go."

"I hope you get what you deserve. Get lost, you bastard. I should've never come here with you!"

Nick opened the door of the apartment and tossed his bag out.

"Take my name off this fucking lease. You're on your own."

"   Good riddance!"

Nick slammed the door causing the whole apartment to tremble. As soon as he was gone, Janice got dressed and stormed out of the apartment. She wanted to go someplace, but her anger had her mind spinning in all directions. Finally, Janice caught a taxi to the subway station and rode it to Georgetown. As soon as she got off, Janice went into the coffee shop she'd visited before. She ordered a drink, sat down at a table in the corner of the shop, and cried.

28

The Clarity of Being Single (2 Months Later)

Things were getting bad for Janice, and she was starting to become afraid. She didn't realize that rent would eat so much of her paycheck. Although Janice could handle most of the expenses, she was surprised at how other things ate away her money. There was the cell phone bill, water, electricity, transportation to and from work, and food. With winter approaching and the cost of electricity creeping higher and higher, she began to contemplate moving.

To compound her problems, Janice started smoking more and more. Outside of work, she stopped going out of the house and told herself that she would use the time she spent at home to focus more on her painting. But after taking a few puffs of weed, all her energy disappeared, and Janice found herself lying around the apartment high, unable to focus.

On the weekends, she found herself deep in depression, wondering where Nick was and what he was doing. Janice tried telling herself she didn't miss him, but that was a lie that never held up to the apartment's loneliness. Nick used to call her to say hello from time to time. Occasionally he sent money to her for his portion of the bills he skated out on, but Janice didn't expect him to continue doing that, and eventually, he stopped. After a few weeks, Nick's phone calls stopped too. Janice had no idea of where he lived or if he was even in the city anymore. The only thing she knew for sure was that they weren't together.

As time went on, Janice became lost in the city with no real friends and no one to comfort her. She stopped hanging out with Scarlett because she discovered that her supposed friend was more self-serving than she pretended to be. Scarlett had told the truth about being in school but failed to admit to being a drug dealer. Scarlett supplemented her income by selling drugs to her friends, and by the time Janice figured it all out, she was another customer copping weed regularly.

One day Janice got off from work early and decided to stop by Scarlett's to pick up her usual dime bag. As soon as she climbed out of the taxi in front of Scarlett's house, she knew something was wrong. There were men's boxers and t-shirts covering the bushes in front of the brownstone. Suddenly a tall, lanky man dressed in a gray business suit pushed open the front door, yelling back into the house.

"Look at this shit! You didn't have to throw all my clothes out on the lawn for the whole neighborhood to see."

Janice stood outside the cab watching as the man picked up his pieces of clothing. Seconds later, Scarlett appeared at the door yelling and screaming.

"You stupid son of a bitch!"

"I'll be by for the rest of my things tomorrow."

"Yeah? They'll be burning in the front yard when you come back."

The man's eyes finally fell on Janice, watching from the side of the street.

"Hi, Janice."

"Hi, Greg."

"I'm sorry about all this."

Janice looked away as Greg threw his clothes into the passenger side of his luxury car and walked around to get into the other side. Just as he pulled away, Scarlett came out of the house. Several neighbors watched the action from the safety of their front porches, and Scarlett lit into them.

"What the fuck are you all looking at? Mind your goddamned business!"

Scarlett finally saw Janice.

"You coming in?"

Janice ambled behind Scarlett into the house. Once the women were inside, Scarlett slammed the door.

"Oh my fucking God, I hate men!"

Janice was reluctant to ask the dam-bursting question. Still, she did it anyway.

"What was that about?"

"Omelets and student loans."

"What?"

"That son of a bitch forgot to pay my student loan."

"Oh."

"I had to pay out of my pocket."

"But...isn't that's what's supposed to happen anyway?"

"We had an agreement. I pay the small bills, and Greg pays the big ones. Greg didn't keep up his side of the bargain."

Scarlett got up and walked to the small desk in the corner. She opened one of the drawers and pulled out a medium-sized velvet bag.

"You came to re-up?" Scarlett asked as she opened the bag.

"Yeah. My usual."

Scarlett took out two clear plastic bags and placed them on the desk.

"Can you believe that son of a bitch threw an omelet at me?"

"Oh, that's what you mean by omelets and student loans."

"I spent all morning making a nice breakfast for the two of us, and he took the omelet and threw it at me."

Scarlett pointed to the greasy stain on the dining room wall.

"Fuck him. I can be late on bills without his help."

Janice nodded and tried to change the subject.

"That last bag you gave me was weak."

"I know. I was trying this new guy that bragged about how good it was. I won't be getting any more of his stuff."

Scarlett passed one of the puffy bags to Janice, and Janice gave her some folded bills. Their exchange was seamless, and they continued talking as if the transaction never took place.

"How's life without the Rockstar?"

"I'm okay."

"You got a new guy in mind yet?"

"No. I just couldn't take the drama. I'm just trying to figure things out on my own, you know?"

"Yeah. But nothing helps you forget a guy better than getting a new one. You should probably think about going out again. Unless you're trying to be one of those ten-cat ladies ordering vibrators online."

Janice didn't appreciate Scarlett's comment. Who was she to give her advice? Scarlett had just thrown her boyfriend's clothes into the street.

"Well...shouldn't you be following your advice? From the looks of it, you're no better off than I am," Janice finally said. Scarlett stared angrily at Janice. Finally, she broke into laughter.

"You're so right, girl. I can't throw shit without getting it on my hands."

Scarlett grabbed her velvet bag and went to sit on the sofa beside Janice.

"I need to clear the cobwebs out of my head. Weed's not strong enough for me today."

Scarlett dropped two black pills into her palm and grabbed a bottle of water from the coffee table. She placed the drugs on her tongue and took a big gulp of water.

"What's that?" asked Janice.

"My special concoction for hard times."

"What does it do?"

"It pushes all of your stress out of your body through your toes. It's delicious! Do you want to try a couple?"

"No. I'm not into anything heavy."

"Yeah. I forgot. You're queen chick shit when it comes to trying new things."

Janice blushed and looked away.

"I am not."

"Remember when you smoked for the first time? You were like a babe in the woods. And that was only weed. No way you're big enough to try something like this."

"What is this, the hard sell?"

"I don't sell this stuff. As I said, I made this. It's mine."

"I don't think so."

Scarlett placed two pills inside of a napkin and passed them to Janice.

"Take these for later. It's probably better if you're home anyway. You want to be in a safe place in case you start tripping."

Reluctantly, Janice took the pills and put them into her purse.

"I'll take them, but I doubt I'll use them."

"Keep them for a rainy day. You never know."

Janice stood and walked to the front door.

"I have to get home. I'll talk to you a little later in the week."

"Okay. See you later."

As soon as Janice got home, she took the plastic bag out of her purse and put it in her suitcase. She placed the black pills on the kitchen counter and sat down to watch her favorite tv show. After a few minutes, her cell phone rang.

"Hello?" asked Janice.

"Who is this?" asked a female voice.

Janice was confused and stuttered a bit in her response.

"W-what?"

"Who is this?"

"You called me. I didn't call you."

"How do you know my man?"

"What?"

"You heard me. Why is your phone number in my man's cell phone?"

Janice felt a cold lump in her throat.

"I don't know. Who is *your* man?"

"You know who my man is, bitch."

"No, I don't."

But Janice could guess who the girl was – Nick's new girlfriend. Her heart broke into a thousand pieces.

"Why does Nicky have your phone number?" asked the girl.

Janice could hear several other women in the background pushing the girl for confrontation.

"Nicky?" asked Janice.

The name sounded so childish that she had a hard time imagining Nick allowing someone to call him by such a name.

"Stay the hell away from my man!"

"Fuck you!"

Janice hung up the phone and threw it across the room. Her eyes suddenly fell on a picture of the two of them – a photo she'd taken on their bus ride to the city. Janice stood and snatched the picture frame from the table and broke it on the floor. Tears streamed down her face as she stared at the photo lying amongst the broken glass on the floor.

"You stupid son of a bitch! I want you out of my life forever!" she yelled.

In the photo, Nick's smile seemed to be laughing at her. She reached down and snatched the picture from the floor, slicing her thumb open in the process. But Janice never felt the injury. She ripped the photo into a million pieces and threw it into the trashcan. Next, Janice went through the apartment searching for everything that Nick had ever given her. When she finished gathering those things, she placed them all in a large bag and took them to the trash room for disposal.

When she returned to her apartment, Janice's eyes fell on the pills sitting on the counter. She went into the kitchen, put the pills in her mouth, and grabbed a bottle of water. After swallowing the drugs, she went to her bed and waited for the feeling to rush over her. It didn't take long.

Another Six Months Behind You

"You wanted to see me, Julie?"

"Yeah. Come on in and sit down. Close the door behind you."

Janice walked into the office and closed the door. She sat down in the empty chair in front of her manager's desk.

"Is something wrong?"

"I just wanted to have a sit-down with you to make sure everything is okay. How are things going?"

"Everything's great so far."

"No issues at home?"

"No. Nothing unusual. Why do you ask?"

"One of my duties as a supervisor is to anticipate issues before they become full-blown problems. You've called out sick four times this month."

"Oh...that."

"Overall, your performance has been above average. No one has made any complaints about you. We want to make sure it stays that way. Is there any way I can be of assistance?"

"The callouts were because I had to move. My boyfriend and I broke up, and I had to downgrade because of the budget problems."

"Oh, I'm sorry to hear that. Did you have family in the area to help you move?"

"No. I live alone in the city."

"That sucks. If you had let us know, some of us would've gone to help you out. I know I would've. I'm not great at lifting beds and dressers, but I'm okay with lifting a box or two."

Janice and Julie both giggled.

"Thanks. I appreciate the offer. If I move again, I'll take you up on that."

There was a moment of strained silence in the room. Finally, Julie cleared her throat and spoke again.

"When was the last time you went to the doctor for a checkup?"

The question surprised Janice, causing her to shift uncomfortably in her chair.

"Sorry, I don't understand your question."

"Janice, it's not easy for me to ask such a thing, but I have to. The weight loss. Have you gone to a doctor to see what's wrong?"

"I've dropped a few pounds, but it's nothing out of the ordinary. And...why are you even asking me something like this? The question seems really out of bounds."

"It's not my intention to give you a difficult time. It's just..."

Janice angrily interrupted Julie.

"I do my job better than anyone around here. I don't understand why you guys are giving me such a hard time."

"We've been avoiding questioning you about it."

"We? Who's we?"

"Well, the whole team."

"I've only heard you asking the uncomfortable questions. Nobody else has said anything to me about it."

"I'm not trying to blame you for anything, Janice. We're just worried. The weight loss, the bloodshot eyes, the callouts. Look at things from my point of view."

"Everything's fine!"

Julie sighed and sat back in her chair.

"Okay. Everything's fine. That's all I wanted to discuss. You can go."

Janice stood and walked out of the office. As she walked to the coatroom, a few of her colleagues cast looks in her direction as if they'd heard the conversation she just had. Janice ignored them. She grabbed her coat, clocked out of the time clock, and left.

As soon as the cold air hit Janice's face, her heart started racing. She was happy to be off work and sprinted down the street to her bus stop as fast as she could. Julie's questioning made her nervous. Now everyone at work knew her secret and would start asking a lot of questions.

"Nosey bitch!" Janice grumbled as she arrived at the same time as her bus.

After flashing her bus pass, she climbed on board and found a seat next to the window. As Janice looked out at two teenagers running beside the bus to get the driver's attention, she thought about the conversation with her supervisor. Janice didn't understand the reason her boss felt comfortable enough to ask those kinds of questions. Wasn't there a law that prevented supervisors from asking personal questions like those?

Although she hadn't run much, beads of sweat were on her forehead. As the bus pulled away from the bus stop, she internally wished the vehicle would move faster. Suddenly, she jumped and smacked at the back of her neck. It felt like a spider had fallen on the base of her neck and crawled down her back. Janice looked around to see if anyone noticed her unease. Aside from a little boy that couldn't take his eyes off her, no one had noticed. Without realizing what she was doing, Janice started clicking her tongue. She was trying to take her mind off the tremendous hunger gnawing at her insides. Her empty stomach sucked in against her ribs, emitting an embarrassing growling noise that everyone could hear. She licked her dry, chapped lips and looked out the window. The bus had only gone half a block.

"Shit! Why is the driver driving so slow?" Janice growled.

After an eternity of waiting, the bus finally pulled up in front of the subway. Janice ran to the escalator and looked at the long metal stairs stretching down into blackness. As she approached, a sudden urge to vomit came over her. She bent over a metal trashcan and hurled. The only thing that came out was a clear liquid. Thankful she hadn't eaten lunch, Janice wiped her mouth and dug into her purse.

"I'd better get a cab. There's no way I'm going to make it on a subway."

Janice ran to the corner and raised a hand in the air to hail a taxi. Seconds later, she climbed into the car on her way to see Scarlett.

When the taxi finally pulled up to Scarlett's house, Janice could hardly contain herself. The pain was excruciating, and she passed the money to the driver without waiting for change. Janice dashed up the stairs and rang the doorbell. She only waited a couple of seconds before ringing again. Only a brief moment passed, and she banged with her fists.

"Scarlett! Open up! It's me!"

An old lady sitting on the porch of the house beside Scarlett's spoke up.

"She's not there."

"She's not there? What do you mean? Where is she?"

Janice could hardly stand in one place. She moved from side to side and kept looking into the windows of the house.

"She's been gone for a few hours."

"A few hours? Did she say when she'd be back?"

"Not for a while. The cops took her away."

"The cops?"

"Yeah. The police made a big fuss about it too. Those cops stomped all over everything and took a lot of bags out of her house."

"Well...what about her boyfriend, Greg? Where is he?"

"He moved out. I haven't seen him since Scarlett threw his stuff out into the street."

Janice's body felt like melted butter - her legs had no strength, and she could barely control her movements. She turned away from the house and walked down the street. After hailing a taxi, she went home.

30

Next Level

Janice's new apartment wasn't new at all. It was inside an old four-story brick building in Woodley Park, a part of the city with a lot of crime. There were no friendly neighbors and trendy coffee shops, only shady individuals and fast-food restaurants. An excessive number of police cars patrolled the apartment building's surrounding streets to make residents feel safe. However, instead of feeling safe, the constant police presence had the opposite effect and made Janice feel like the apartment building was in a warzone.

There were overflowing garbage cans in front of the apartment building that the garbage collectors either continuously overlooked every week or couldn't empty fast enough. The bus stop in front of the apartment building usually had a homeless man laid across the bench, forcing Janice to walk one block down the street to wait at the other bus stop when she needed to take the bus.

It was nighttime when Janice pulled up in front of her building and climbed out. A group of teenagers was gathered out front, arguing and joking with one another.

"I'm telling you, man, Craig's going to take them all the way. He's the best player on their whole squad."

"Yeah, but one person doesn't win a game. They're going to lose, and you know it."

"Put your money where your mouth is, bitch. Twenty says they don't make it past the first round."

"That's easy money. I've got to take that. You're on."

Janice looked through the boys to the entrance.

"Excuse me," she said as she walked through the middle of the group blocking the stairway. The boys moved out of the way and stopped talking. As soon as Janice tapped in her code to enter the building, the boys continued to talk.

"Steve told me Craig hurt his foot during the summer. He's not going to be able to put in a lot of minutes during the tournament."

Janice walked into the building and down the hall. Just as she was about to put her key in the door, a thought occurred to her. She walked back to the front door and opened it to speak to the group of teenagers, but they were gone.

"Fuck!" she cursed.

Janice took a couple of steps out of the apartment building and peered down the sidewalk. There were a couple of men with hoodies standing in the shadows of the streetlight a half-block away. Janice was afraid of what she was contemplating, and she wanted to go to her apartment. But the hunger inside her was making her stomach do backflips. Even if she turned around and went into the apartment, her pains would have her back outside before night's end. Janice took one final look down the street and started walking.

As soon as Janice arrived in front of the two men, she began to shake.

"Hey. Are you guys holding?"

One of the men turned away from her and started to walk away.

"Are you a fucking cop or something?" asked the other guy as he turned to walk away too.

"No...I just need to buy some weed."

The guy paused and lowered his hoodie to stare at Janice.

"You've got the shakes."

"I'm a little sick, is all. I've got the flu."

"You've got the flu, and you're out here at night trying to cop? You sure you're only out here for weed?"

"Yeah. I mean unless you've got something stronger."

The man chuckled and shook his head.

"I knew it. Like what?"

"You got base?"

"How much cash do you have?"

Janice dug into her pocket and pulled out a $50.

"You got some?"

"Whoa, whoa. What the fuck are you doing? Don't give that to me."

The man pointed across the street.

"Give that to the guy on the corner and walk to the end of the block and wait. Someone will serve you."

"Okay. Thanks."

Janice crossed the street and walked up to the boy leaning against the building. She passed him her money and watched as the boy took off running. Seconds later, a kid that seemed no older than 7 or 8 ran up to her and gave her a red-topped vile. As soon as he dropped it in her hand, the boy took off running and disappeared into the night.

Excited and barely able to contain herself, Janice put the small container into her pants pocket and walked back to her apartment building. She entered her code and ran into the building. As Janice fumbled to put her key into her door, a tall man watched her from the other end of the apartment hallway. But Janice didn't care. Her mind was focused on one thing – stopping the pain. Finally, she got her key into the lock and opened her apartment door. As she entered, she looked back down the hall to see if the man was still watching her. He was gone. Janice shut her door and locked it. Five minutes later, she was drooling as she sat in front of her television, all her pain gone.

31

Lightning in the Clouds

"Stacy, can you cover for me? I need to run to the bathroom."

"Sure thing, Janice."

Janice left the cash register and walked quickly to the bathroom. She pushed open the nearest bathroom stall, dropped her pants, and sat down quickly. Liquid splashed into the toilet, sending a foul odor into the air. Janice could feel the inside of her stomach burning. She stood and looked into the toilet bowl – it was filled with blood. After taking several deep breaths, Janice wiped herself and flushed the toilet. She walked out of the stall to the sink with her pants down around her ankles. Janice spotted a broom in the corner of the bathroom and shuffled over to grab it. After fumbling around, she slid the handle of the broom between the metal lock and the doorknob. Satisfied that no one could enter the bathroom, Janice went back to the sink, ran warm water, and cleaned herself thoroughly with wet paper towels.

By the time Janice got back to the cash register, there were customers everywhere. Her coworker Stacy was sweating furiously. The line in front of her stretched to the entrance and almost out the door.

"Sorry. I wasn't feeling well," Janice explained as she unlocked her cash register.

Stacy was angry and yelled at the customers.

"Everyone from the gentleman in the hat, please move over to this register so that we can help you," she said, directing customers to Janice's register.

Half the line obediently moved and waited for Janice to call the first customer.

"I'll take the next customer," Janice said while looking around to see if anyone was watching.

Stacy was busy ringing up a customer, and there wasn't another salesperson on the floor. Janice quickly opened her register, removed three $20 bills, and shoved them into her pocket. When she looked up, she was surprised – standing in front of her was the man from her apartment building! Unsure of how to react, Janice pretended to search for something on the counter to her left. Finally realizing she couldn't ignore the man forever, Janice looked at him.

"Hi. Can I help you?" Janice asked.

"I'll take these two books, please," the man responded.

Janice was surprised at the deepness of the man's voice. It sounded like smooth thunder pouring out of his mouth. The man was more attractive than she remembered. His brown hair was neatly trimmed and nicely styled. He was wearing a delicious cologne that Janice never smelled before – a mixture of exotic spices and fresh apples.

Janice looked at the books the man wanted to purchase.

"These are pretty good. I've read these books."

The man remained silent. Janice looked around to see if her supervisor was nearby. Feeling uncomfortable about what the man had witnessed, Janice tried to engage the man in light conversation again.

"I've seen you somewhere, haven't I?"

"We live in the same building."

Janice feigned surprise.

"Really? I never would've guessed."

The man cracked a slight smile.

"How much do I owe you?"

Janice scanned the two books.

"That'll be $32.40."

The man pulled cash from his wallet and passed it to Janice.

"Well, I guess we'll see each other in the apartment building," Janice said as she passed the bag of books to the man.

"Sure. Thanks," the man said and walked towards the exit.

Janice stared at the man as he moved through the crowd. She marveled at the strange man's behavior. He'd witnessed her stealing from the store, yet he never mentioned it.

"Weird," Janice said underneath her breath.

Before he left the store, the man stopped and turned around to look at Janice. Their eyes met, and he smiled before finally leaving the store.

32

Descent

It was almost 1 am when Janice decided to leave her apartment. The time didn't bother her because she'd practically stopped sleeping altogether. The only thing she could think of was her next fix. The hunger inside her had become something more uncontrollable - a demon of torture that clawed at her from the inside, inflicting intense chest and abdominal pain. Janice had started taking large amounts of drugs, but her highs no longer stopped or even kept the pain at bay. Still, Janice was on a constant search for relief.

As she exited her apartment building and stepped out into the foggy night, she looked down the street and saw two shadows standing underneath the streetlight.

"Good. Dougie's working," whispered Janice.

She'd learned his name by accident when a kid ran up to him when she was there. At first, he'd gotten angry and cursed the child. But as time went on and he saw how profitable Janice became, he didn't mind. He only cared about the cash she would bring him. That was cool with Janice because she only cared about the redtops he had in his possession.

As Janice got closer to the shadows standing underneath the streetlight, she paused. The two figures were ones she didn't recognize. She thought about turning around and going back to her apartment. Janice didn't want anything to happen to her. Suddenly, as if sensing her apprehension, a pain in her chest made her body jerk in agony. Obediently, she listened to the monster's complaints and continued walking to buy what she needed. As soon as she arrived in front of the men, Janice got right to the point.

"Where's Dougie?" she asked.

The men were older than the guys she usually saw. These two guys looked dirty and unclean. One of the guys had a rough beard sprinkled with grey hair. The other guy was younger and had a scar on his lip that stretched to his chin.

"Who?" asked the older man.

"Dougie. Are you guys taking his place? I need to cop some base."

The younger guy moved closer to Janice.

"Dougie? Yeah, yeah. We're taking his place."

"What do you have?"

"Everything. Base. Is that all you need?"

"Yeah. Just a couple of vials."

"Yeah, we have that. But it's around the corner."

The man pointed to an ally half a block away from them.

"There? You don't have runners?"

The young man started laughing.

"Funny shit. The cops came and shut us down earlier and chased our runners away. Now we have to sell the stuff ourselves."

Janice looked at the men suspiciously and then glanced down the street at the alley.

"I don't know."

"What's wrong? You want to get high, don't you? Why are you afraid? You have money, and we have the product. It's a simple transaction."

After considering what the man said, Janice decided to take a chance.

"You guys lead. I'll follow you."

"Sure thing, cutie. It's right over here."

The two men led Janice to the alley and entered while she paused at the entrance.

"Come on. It's right in here," said the guy with the scar. Suddenly Janice's fear became too big for her to ignore. She took two steps back.

"I don't think so."

The other guy stuck his hand into an opening on the side of the building and pulled out a plastic bag filled with small vials of drugs.

"You see? We're not bullshitting you."

Once again, the pain inside Janice's chest took over, making her heartbeat pound in her ears. She took another step into the alley.

"You got the money?" the younger guy asked while extending his open hand holding one plastic container.

Janice dug into her jeans and pulled out her money. As she looked down to unfold it, both men rushed toward her. Janice tried to scream, but one of the men put his hand over her mouth.

"Quick! Hit that bitch before someone hears her!"

Janice didn't know which one struck her, but the crunch of knuckles on her jawbone made her blackout temporarily. As soon as her knees hit the ground, she woke up moaning. One of the men hit her again. This time it was a blow to her stomach. All the air in her lungs rushed out, and Janice struggled to catch her breath. The men dropped her into a puddle of water beside a metal dumpster. As Janice laid gasping for air, she felt the men rummaging through her pockets.

"She got anything?"

"Nothing! Just another $20. Fucking bitch!"

Janice felt the man's boot kick her in the mouth, spinning her head in the opposite direction and causing her neck to pop. The pain was excruciating. Janice was sure one of her front teeth had gone through her top lip and was leaking blood all over the ground.

"We should rape your stupid ass for wasting our time like this," the guy complained.

Suddenly Janice heard a belt buckle.

"Yeah! Let's do it! Let's rape this bitch!" said his friend unzipping his pants.

Janice's eyes widened.

"No...no...no.." she cried over and over.

Suddenly her eyes fell on a metal rod lying on the ground beside the trashcan.

"Turn that bitch over. I'm going first!"

"Fuck you! It was my idea to rob her!"

"Okay, but hurry up!"

The man grabbed Janice's arm and attempted to turn her over. Just as he did, Janice grabbed the pole from the ground and shoved it into the man's groin.

The man didn't scream. There was only a look of surprise on his face as he shivered and fell on top of Janice. She could feel his warm blood drenching her pants.

"Hey, what are you doing? Get up so I can get my turn," said his friend as he rushed forward.

He lifted his friend off Janice.

"Holy fucking shit!" he whispered as he saw the blood pouring out of him. "You bitch!"

The man pulled a gun from his waist and aimed it at Janice's face. Just as he was about to pull the trigger, a hand reached out and twisted his arm into his abdomen.

"What the fuck..."

A loud pop rang out, and the drug dealer fell on top of his bleeding friend with a blank look on his face. Janice looked up and saw the man from her building standing in front of her. He extended his hand to her.

"Don't speak. Listen. Go straight to your apartment and stay there until I clean this up. I shouldn't be longer than 30 minutes."

Janice couldn't move. Although the alley was dark, she could still see the eyes of both of the men lying on the ground – dead.

"What am I going to do? I killed someone! I need to go to the police!"

"Calm down! Relax! You were only protecting yourself. Do as I say, and you'll be able to put this whole thing behind you."

The man lifted Janice from the ground and led her to the alley's entrance. After looking both ways, he pushed her out onto the sidewalk.

"Go. I'll be there shortly."

Janice tried running up the street, but she felt a dull pain in her back. Her head was pounding, and everything seemed to be moving. She knew her left eye was swollen shut, and her top lip felt like a balloon in the night air. Still, she kept her head down and continued walking until she reached her apartment building entrance. She entered her code, went inside, and froze – her house keys! She'd forgotten that the men had taken everything out of her pants in the alley. Janice wanted to go back outside to get the keys to her apartment, but she was too afraid. She was too scared of seeing the murdered men. Janice placed her back against her door and slid down to the ground. She put her head down between her knees and waited. Hopefully, no one would notice her blood-soaked pants.

It wasn't long before her neighbor returned from the alley. As soon as Janice saw him, she stood up in front of her door.

"I don't have my keys," she whispered through tears.

The man reached into his pocket and pulled out some keys.

"Here you go. I found your keys on the ground."

"Thank you! Thank you!"

Janice snatched the keys from the man's hands and unlocked her door. She ran into the apartment and left the door open for the man to enter. He stayed outside the door and didn't enter.

"Hey. Aren't you coming in?"

"I need to clean up. You do too. Take a shower and put everything you were wearing into a plastic bag. I'll be back after I clean up."

The man turned and started walking down the hall. Janice stuck her head out the door.

"Hey! Hey!"

The man turned and looked at Janice.

"I don't know your name."

"Carl."

As the man walked away, Janice shut the door of her apartment and did as Carl had told her.

33

Criminals

Janice was looking out of her apartment window with a wet towel pressed to her face when she heard a light knock at the door. She tiptoed across the room and looked out through the peephole.

"Who is it?" she asked softly.

"It's Carl."

Janice quickly unlocked the door, and Carl walked into the apartment. He was wearing different clothes, and he smelled of bleach.

"Did you clean everything?" Janice asked nervously. "Did you get rid of the bodies? What about the cops?"

Carl saw a large garbage bag sitting next to the door.

"I see you got the clothes. You put everything in here?"

"Yeah."

"Shoes? Underwear?"

"Yeah. Everything's there."

Carl lifted the bag, tied it, and dropped it in front of the door. He took Janice's chin in his hand and looked at her face.

"You took a beating out there. You have a hole in your lip, and you're probably going to need stitches."

Suddenly a thought flashed through Janice's head.

"My blood! It's probably all over the ground!"

Carl let go of Janice's face and grabbed the garbage bag.

"No, it's not. I took my time. The alley is clean."

"But how did you..."

"Don't worry about all that. We don't have a lot of time. Do you have some thread and a needle?"

"For what?"

"I've got to sew you up before we get out of here. It makes no sense to run when you're dripping blood everywhere."

"Where are we going?"

"Did you sign a lease?"

"No."

"Neither did I. When we leave, there won't be much to track back to us. I'll have to come back and clean the apartment after you're gone, but don't you worry about that."

Janice stared at the man.

"Who are you?"

"I told you my name."

"Yeah, but why are you doing all of this for me?"

The man shook his head and grabbed the bag.

"You ask a lot of questions."

"Wouldn't you?"

"I wouldn't have been in a dark alley with two strange men trying to score some drugs at 1 am. The best time to ask questions would've been before you ended up there."

Embarrassed, Janice turned away from Carl.

"I'll get rid of these and grab a few things from my apartment. I'll be back in a few minutes."

As soon as Carl left the apartment, Janice became terrified. The walls were closing in, and it was only a matter of time before the police figured out who did the crime. Maybe she should make a run for it.

Just as Janice was about to run out the door, it opened, and Carl came back in. He was carrying a large paper bag.

"You got something to drink?"

"If I did, do you think I would've been out there?"

"I figured as much."

Carl dug into the bag and pulled out a bottle of vodka. He took off the cap, took a big gulp, and passed the bottle to Janice.

"Drink this."

"What is it?"

"Seeing as how you've been doing drugs, this probably won't have much effect on you. Drink as much vodka as your throat can stand, and then I'll get started."

Janice took a big gulp of the alcohol. It burned like fire going down her throat, and Janice almost sprayed the vodka onto the floor. After pausing to catch her breath, she took another deep gulp. Her whole body started warming, and that hunger she felt for drugs briefly disappeared. Carl took the bottle from her.

"Now get me an ice cube," instructed Carl.

Janice walked to the kitchen and returned with a tray of ice cubes.

"Lay down on the bed."

Janice laid on the bed and winced as Carl placed an ice cube directly on the gash in her lip.

"This is going to hurt. Close your eyes."

As soon as the needle went into her lip, Janice almost screamed.

"Relax. Let the alcohol do its job."

But Janice couldn't contain herself. She never realized the needle would be so painful.

"How many times are you sticking me? This shit hurts!"

"Unless you want stitches on your nose, I suggest you stop talking."

Janice stopped talking and remained silent until Carl finished. When he finished, she attempted to sit up and almost tumbled off the bed.

"Easy," said Carl as he helped her off the bed.

He stood in the middle of the floor and looked around.

"Do you have anything you want to take with you?"

Janice started laughing. Carl ignored her and gathered the bloody towels. He tucked them into his brown bag and tucked them underneath his arm.

"Let's go."

"Go where?"

"Unless you want to be around when the cops come asking questions, I suggest you get moving."

Janice and Carl walked out of the apartment and locked the door. As soon as they walked out of the building, Janice saw a red SUV.

"Who is that?"

"My wife."

"Your wife?"

Janice was surprised. She didn't realize a married man would be willing to risk everything to save her. The woman rolled down the passenger window and yelled at them.

"Hurry up, honey. The sun's about to come up."

Carl opened the door for Janice and allowed her to sit in the front seat.

"Hello. You must be Janice. Hi Janice, I'm Tonya."

Janice stared at the woman without speaking. Her country drawl threw her off. Tonya smiled politely and looked into the rearview mirror.

"Where are we heading, babe?" Tonya asked Carl.

"I don't know. Home maybe?" he responded.

"Home it is."

The curly-headed blonde woman pulled out onto the street and accelerated.

"Are you going to be sick, Janice?"

"No. I'm fine."

"Do you need a little something to tie you over? We don't truck with hardcore drugs, but I have a couple of pretty strong valiums. It'll help you sleep."

"No, thank you."

The woman ignored Janice and opened the pillbox on the dashboard.

"Carl, can you pass her that bottle of water on the backseat?"

Carl fumbled until he found the bottle. He held it out for Janice to take.

"I said I didn't want anything," she protested.

"Girl, you're far from the land of *what you want* right now. Take the valium or get out and do your own thing."

Janice frowned and popped the pills into her mouth. She did want to take the valiums, but she didn't want to let the strange woman know. She took a sip of water and tossed the bottle into the backseat.

"Now. Was that so freaking hard?" asked Tonya.

"Whatever," responded Janice as she closed her eyes.

As soon as she did, she saw the two drug dealers' faces in the alley. Frightened by seeing the dead men, she opened her eyes again and decided to stay awake, looking out into the city. The sun was rising as the vehicle weaved through the roads. Janice began thinking about Nick. She wondered if he would even care to know what she'd experienced. Although she still saw the girls Nick cheated with vividly in her memory, Nick's face was like a ghost floating between them. Time and the drugs were melting away her memory, and it was becoming harder to remember Nick's face. Their argument seemed like it happened years ago.

Soon Janice's eyelids became too heavy, and she drifted off to sleep.

34

Sign of Power

"Janice? You awake?"

Janice heard a voice calling out to her. For some reason, she couldn't open her eyes. It felt like the world around her was alive and moving, but she could not pull herself out of the depths of slumber.

"Why isn't she waking up?"

"Give the medicine some time to kick in. She should wake up momentarily."

Slowly, Janice began blinking her eyes. Everything was blurry. Soon she saw dark shadows standing all around her.

"Janice, this is Dr. Jenkins. Can you see me?" one of the shadows said.

Janice blinked her eyes a few more times. Soon she was able to make out the faces of the people standing around her.

"Where...where am I?" Janice asked the old grey-haired man standing above her.

"Janice?" called out a voice.

Janice recognized that voice. It was her mom.

"Mom?"

"That's right, baby. It's mommy."

"Where am I? What's going on?"

"You're in the hospital, baby."

Janice's eyes finally adjusted, and she saw her mother standing to her left. Overcome with emotion; she started crying.

"Mom. I don't want…"

Janice's mom kissed her cheek and rubbed her head.

"Shhhh. Don't talk. You need to get your rest."

Janice attempted to lift her hand to touch her mother's face and was surprised to find both her hands strapped down.

"What is this? Why are my hands strapped down?"

The doctor moved in close to Janice.

"We've strapped your hands down for your protection and the staff's protection."

Although she was still groggy, Janice began to get angry.

"What is this shit? Why are you treating me like a criminal? Do you think I'm some kind of psycho or something?"

The doctor ignored Janice's anger.

"What kind of drugs have you been taking?"

Janice's eyes shot to her mother's face.

"Drugs? What drugs? I don't take drugs."

The doctor lifted a clipboard and started writing.

"Do you remember what kind of drugs you took?"

"I told you. I don't take drugs."

The doctor nodded to Janice's mother, and she kissed Janice's cheek.

"I'm going to be going now. We'll visit again in two weeks."

Janice's eyes widened in surprise.

"Two weeks?! What kind of place is this? What did you do?"

Janice's mother backed away from her and turned to walk out the door.

"Mom! Wait! Don't go!" said Janice as she turned to the doctor. "Okay! There was this guy that gave me a few valiums. His name was Carl. Those are the only drugs I've taken. That's it!"

The doctor wrote on his clipboard again, and Janice's mother closed the door behind her.

"Mom!" Janice screamed out. "Don't leave me here! What did you do?"

The doctor pressed a button on the side of Janice's bed.

"Calm down, Janice. You're in good hands."

"What is this place? Why am I here? Let me go!"

Suddenly two male nurses appeared, one of them holding a needle in his hands.

"No! I don't want it! What are you doing?"

The doctor stepped back and let the nurses administer the medicine.

"This is just something to calm you down. Relax, Janice. Relax."

As the medicine took effect, Janice stopped fighting. Her breathing became steadier, and she began to doze off.

"Not...supposed to be...here. Where's...Carl? Mom...what did you...do?"

Finally, she fell asleep.

35

2 Months Later

"You look good. You're putting on some weight."

Janice cracked a little smile as she sat across from her mother.

"I still say this was unnecessary. It's not like I was shooting up with needles or anything."

"Well, you're here, right? The goal is to get clean."

Janice stared at her mom, unsure of her feelings. On the one hand, she was mad as hell about her mom putting her into a drug recovery program. The whole thing felt invasive. Who was she to alter her trajectory as an adult? But then Janice remembered all she'd gone through to get clean, the chills, the hunger, the nightmares.

"What is Trevor up to?" Janice asked.

"Nothing. Your brother's wasting his time playing and reading those stupid comic books. He almost gave me a heart attack the other day. Trevor did a weird backflip on the jungle gym, and I thought for sure that boy would kill himself. But he landed on his feet! Can you believe that?"

"Yeah. Trevor started doing those backflips in front of me – before I moved out."

The two women sat silently for a few moments before Janice's mother started talking again.

"The doctors told me you're going to get out in two weeks. You ready?"

"Yes."

"Good. We have your room all set up and ready for you. It was Trevor's idea to redecorate it, so don't get mad at me if you don't like it."

"I'm sure it'll be fine."

There was another uncomfortable pause.

"How are you able to afford to keep me in this place, mom?"

"What do you mean?"

"I know it costs an arm and a leg, and Michael's too cheap to foot the bill for it. How are you able to pay for it?"

"I'm not paying for it."

"Who is?"

"Your father. It's the least that deadbeat could pay. He's lucky I don't take his ass to court."

Janice's mouth dropped open, and she stared at her mother in disbelief.

"My father? But...how? What kind of job does he have?"

"That's his business. He's probably selling drugs or something. I didn't ask any questions."

"But I thought you lost contact with him. How did you reconnect?"

"Your job."

"My job?"

"You had me listed as an emergency contact. When you didn't show up to work for a few days, they called me. I became worried, so I tracked your father down, and I called him."

Janice shook her head and stared at the floor. For years, her mother had every opportunity to reach out to her father and chose not to do so. Her reaching out to him during her weakest moment was so unfair. What would he say? What would he think about the life she lived in the city? Janice glared at her mother. She felt more violated than ever.

"How did I get to this place?"

"You don't remember?"

"I remember this guy named Carl and his wife helping me out. That's it. Did they drop me off?"

"Yes."

"Where are they now? I want to at least thank them for helping me out."

"You can reach out to them when you're better. I have the phone numbers."

Janice stood and was about to return to her room when she paused.

"Wait. How did Carl and his wife know your address?"

"Well…"

"Well, what?"

"His name isn't Carl. It's Alex."

"What?"

"That's right. Your father and his wife drove you home."

36

Back Home

Janice was sitting on her bed when she heard a knock at the door.

"Who is it?"

The door opened, and Trevor stuck his small head into the room.

"Janice? Can I come in?"

Janice smiled.

"Sure, Trevor. Come on in," she replied.

It was good to be home with her little brother again. Trevor walked in and sat on the bed beside Janice.

"Are you feeling better now? Mommy told me you were sick from your trip."

"Sure. I feel great!"

"Does that mean you'll be leaving again soon?"

"No. I'm staying home for a while so that I can finish school."

The little boy smiled and dangled his feet from the bed.

"You're staying? For sure?"

"For sure."

Suddenly the child's face became sad.

"Why didn't you tell me you were leaving? I was so sad when you left. I didn't have anyone to play with me."

Janice felt the rush of sadness wash over her. Although she decided to leave with Nick, she didn't consider the impact her sudden absence would have on Trevor.

"I made a mistake, Trevor. I didn't tell you, mom, or your dad. That was very wrong of me, and I'm sorry for doing that. Can you forgive me?"

Trevor looked up at his older sister and smiled.

"I forgive you, Janice. But if you leave again, you have to promise me something."

"What's that?"

"You have to promise to take me with you."

"I can't make that kind of promise to you, Trevor. It wouldn't be right. Don't you think mom would be hurt if we both left?"

"She has daddy to keep her company. They don't need me."

"You're wrong about that, Trevor. Mom would go crazy without you here. You mean everything to her. And you mean everything to your dad too. "

"Oh, he doesn't care. Dad only cares about watching football and drinking beer."

"He does care. I know he has a funny way of showing it, but your dad cares about you a lot. All fathers care about their children."

Janice's last statement echoed in her head, and she lost focus on what Trevor was saying.

All fathers care about their children.

Janice began thinking of all the negative things her mother told her about her father. Janice had heard about how irresponsible her father was and how he wasn't a real man. But when Janice tried reconciling the myth with the man, it didn't add up. Janice's father had not only saved her from drug abuse, but he also murdered a man to stop her from being raped. That didn't sound like a man that didn't care about his daughter.

"Janice? Janice, are you okay?"

Janice snapped back to reality and looked at Trevor.

"I'm sorry, Trevor. What were you saying?"

"Did Nick come back with you?"

"No. Nick decided to stay in Washington, DC."

The boy's eyes lit up.

"Wait, you were in Washington, DC? Cool!"

"Yep."

"What places did you see? Did you see the President? Did you go to the White House? The monument?"

"No, Trevor. I didn't see any of those places."

"Why?"

"I was too busy working."

"And Nick is still there?"

"Yep. That's where Nick is now."

"Is he still your boyfriend?"

"No. Nick and I decided to break up. He needed time to chase his dream."

"I liked Nick. He was cool."

"Yeah, he was cool."

"Anyway, mom told me to tell you dinner is almost ready."

"Okay. Let me wash my hands, and I'll be right out."

Trevor stood up and walked to the door.

"After dinner, do you think we could go to the park? I miss going there with you."

"Sure thing, Trevor."

Trevor walked out of the room while Janice went to the bathroom to wash her hands for dinner.

37

Recall

Janice sat on the front porch with her mother, looking at the fireflies light up in the darkness. Janice's stepfather was sitting in the living room watching sports, and Trevor was in his bedroom playing videogames.

"Did you like that baked chicken tonight?" asked Janice's mother while sipping lemonade.

"Yeah, it was pretty good."

"I got the recipe from Margaret at the school. She swears by the recipe, but I wouldn't say I liked it too much. There were too many onions for my taste."

Janice swatted at a giant mosquito that lit on her ankle.

"You ready?" asked her mom.

Janice brushed the bloody insect off her skin and sat up.

"Ready?"

"Are you ready to have our talk about your father? We haven't discussed anything since I told you about him at rehab."

"I don't know. I guess I'm as ready as I'll ever be."

Shannon turned to face her daughter.

"What do you want to know?"

"Everything that I don't know."

"I didn't know where your father was living until I did an online search for his name. Alexander Ellis is his complete name. When I found out he was living in Washington, DC, I was just as shocked as you. I didn't know the first thing about that city, but I was grateful to God that Alex lived there. Based on what your supervisor told me about your appearance, I knew you were mixed up in drugs in some kind of way. Alex was the only option other than the cops. And with you being so young, I didn't want you to have that stain on your record for the rest of your life. So, I got Alex's home address and phone number, and I called him."

"What kind of work does he do?"

"He didn't say, and I didn't want to know."

"You didn't want to know? What if he was a criminal or something?"

"He wasn't. I found out from the background search that he has a security clearance."

"A security clearance? What does that mean?"

"It means Alex either works for the government or he works for a contractor with government ties. When someone has a security clearance, it means that they have to live a sober life. There's no room for getting thrown in jail for binge drinking and drugs on the weekend. That's why I took the chance to get him involved."

"But you told me you thought he was involved in drugs."

"For a long time, I did believe that. You have to understand. Alex and I did a lot of drugs when we were young. Since he left me, I assumed he carried on with that option. It's not like he was a model of responsibility. But obviously, he chose a different path."

"The lady. His wife. Who is she?"

"When I did a background search, I didn't see a wife in his profile. I just assumed since he showed up with her that the two were married."

"You don't know for certain?"

"No, and I don't want to know. Who Alex chooses to fuck is his business. All I know is that they showed up at the house late at night with you in the passenger seat unconscious. From there, they took you to a drug rehabilitation facility and dropped you off. I didn't ask a whole lot of questions. I was just happy to have you home."

"Did he tell you how he found me?"

"No."

"I'm not sure if it was the drugs or not, but I saw him entering an apartment in my building. He even came by my job."

"Really? Before I reached out to him?"

"I think so. You and I had talked, so things hadn't gotten out of control at that point."

"And he never introduced himself as your father?"

"No. At first, I just thought it was a coincidence. But now I see that his presence wasn't by accident."

"Well, if Alex was living in your apartment building, he was on to who you were long before I called him."

Janice slapped at another mosquito and thought about the situation.

"What do you think it means, mom?"

"There's only one way you're going to know."

"What? Call him?"

"Why not? I think you owe him that much for saving your life. No?"

"I wouldn't know what to say. Also, with the drugs and everything, I'd be too embarrassed."

Janice's mother stood up and turned to go into the house.

"Well, it's your father, and it's your decision when you want to talk to him. When you're ready, I have his telephone number."

38

The Slow Life

Getting back into the swing of things proved more difficult for Janice than she'd thought. The girls who had been her friends went away to college. The few remaining girls heard about her Washington DC adventures, and their parents instructed them to stay away. For months Janice wandered around the town feeling out of place and alone. Malls, Friday nights, and phone calls – they all ceased being outlets for letting off steam, and Janice felt like she would die of loneliness. But eventually, she accepted her new place in her old town and tried to make the best of it.

School also proved to be a challenge. She couldn't just return to her high school to request a do-over after skating out on her excursion during her senior year. Some of the kids in the classes beneath her would know she didn't belong and would ridicule her to no end. After her mother had a conversation with the high school principal, they agreed that the school would allow Janice to receive her assignments and complete them at home. At the end of the school year, Janice would receive her diploma in the mail and avoid the embarrassment of attending the graduation ceremony.

Homelife for Janice wasn't easy either. After her mother and step-father went to work and her brother went off to school, Janice was left alone in the house to do her school assignments. In the beginning, things were simple. Janice could blast her radio and immerse herself in schoolwork until her mother came through the door at 6:00 pm. But it wasn't long before boredom pushed some aspects of the city life she'd lived into her mind. Janice found herself craving some of the things that almost destroyed her, chief among those things being the drugs.

On several occasions, she went into the bathroom medicine cabinet and rummaged through the medicine there. After trying unsuccessfully to stop fantasizing about her past drug use, Janice would go into the bathroom, open random bottles of medication, and place the pills on her tongue. To satisfy her cravings, she rolled the different medicine capsules around her mouth, imagining that they were her favorite drug. One time Janice even swallowed one of her stepfather's blood pressure pills to see if anything would happen. But in the end, the medication only made her nauseous, so she never tried it again.

And so, things went on for Janice, month after month. Sometimes she thought about Nick, and sometimes she didn't. There were moments she was terrified of what happened in the alley with the two drug dealers, and she could barely keep it together. And then, other times, the whole incident seemed like something Janice had seen in a movie. Her father melted away from her immediate thoughts. She couldn't think of him without thinking of what happened with the drug dealers, so she chose to push it all deep down, away from the surface of reality.

39

Rough Roads Revisited

Janice had just finished her calculus assignment and was about to make herself a peanut butter sandwich when the telephone rang.

"Hello?"

There wasn't a response, only the sound of heavy breathing.

"Hello?" Janice asked again.

Still, there was no answer. Frustrated, she hung up the phone and went into the kitchen to make her sandwich. Seconds later, the phone rang again.

"Hello?" Janice asked once more.

Yet again, the person didn't respond.

"Look, you sick pervert. Get a life!"

"Janice?" asked a shaky male's voice. "Is this Janice?"

Janice froze. Although the voice sounded different, she could recognize that voice anywhere. It was Nick.

"Janice. I know you don't want to talk to me, but I'm in trouble and need your help. Please don't..."

"Fuck you."

Janice hung up the phone and went back to making her sandwich. She was surprised at how coldly and quickly she shut down Nick's phone call. Inside she celebrated. Nick needed her. Of all the people in the world, he needed *her*. She imagined Nick somewhere stranded, waiting for her to call him back and suffering on the cold streets when he finally realized that she would never call him back.

"Jerk!" Janice said as she slathered peanut butter on a slice of bread.

Seconds later the phone rang again, but this time Janice didn't answer it. Instead, she went into the den, turned on the television, and ate her sandwich in peace. Although she was happy about ignoring Nick in his moment of need, a part of her was worried. There must've been something severe that compelled Nick to pick up the phone to call her.

The phone started ringing again. This time Janice picked it up.

"What?"

"Janice, don't hang up. Please! I just need..."

Suddenly Nick started coughing uncontrollably. Janice rolled her eyes and shook her head.

"What is it, Nick? I don't have all day."

Finally, Nick stopped coughing.

"Can you come to get me?"

"Get you? Where?"

"I'm in DC at Union Station."

"You act like I have a car and money. Sorry. I'm not traveling to DC ever again."

"Please! I'm begging you! It's serious!"

"First of all, how did you get my number?"

"I just guessed you went back home."

"I'm not going to DC, Nick."

Janice listened as Nick started crying.

"You don't understand. I'm sick."

"Sick?"

"Yeah. The doctors say it's cancer."

Janice sat up on the sofa and turned off the television.

"Cancer? But how? What kind? You're too young to be sick."

"They say it's lung cancer. I don't know how I got it, but the doctors say that's what it is."

"Why didn't you contact your parents? Why me?"

"Because you're the only person that cared about me. My parents don't give a shit. They never did."

"This is bigger than me, Nick. You need to call your parents. I'll contact them if you want me to."

"No! I need you, okay? Just you! Can you come and get me or not?"

"Not."

"Then you would leave me to die?"

Nick started crying again and broke into a new fit of coughing.

"I'm sorry you're sick, but I'm still not traveling to DC. You need to find another way."

Nick stopped coughing and remained silent.

"Nick? You there?"

Finally, Nick spoke.

"Yes, I'm here.

"Did the doctors say how bad it was?"

"They didn't tell me how long I have, but it's terminal. It's not long."

Janice's heart broke into a million pieces. Nick was leaving this world forever, and there wasn't anything she could do to stop it.

"Janice?" asked Nick.

"What is it?" whispered Janice.

Her throat filled with sorrow, and she could barely talk.

"I need to tell you something."

"Go ahead."

"I'm sorry for the way I treated you. I was a cold and heartless prick, only concerned with what I wanted. I never helped you pursue your dreams. I didn't have your back when you needed me."

Janice broke down after hearing Nick's words. She never realized she still loved Nick so much, and his apology made her feel like someone dropped a ton of bricks on her soul.

"No matter the weak excuse I tried to give you, I admit that I was unfaithful to you. I hurt you, and if you choose never to forgive me, I won't blame you. With everything that's happening with me, I just wanted you to know how I felt. If we never see one another again, just know that I am sorry for all the pain I caused you. Goodbye."

Nick's apology touched something deep in Janice that she never knew existed. Perhaps Nick was only playing to her emotions because he was desperate. But the fact that he admitted the pain he'd caused her mattered. And no matter how big of a jerk he'd been, Janice couldn't turn her back on someone she'd been in a relationship with.

"Nick! Wait!"

"Yeah?"

"Union Station?"

"Yes."

"And after I pick you up, where do you want me to take you?"

"I just want to go home quietly without the drama. If my parents knew the truth about me, that ride home would be pure hell. If this is my last bit of time on this earth, I just want to go home in silence, riding beside someone that genuinely cares for me."

Janice thought for a few seconds. Finally, she spoke.

"I'll be there in two days. Friday at 2:00 pm."

"You sure? How will you get here?"

"I'll use my mom's car. Just be there at the taxi stand."

"Okay. Janice?"

"Yes?"

"I love you. Do you still love me?"

The question made Janice feel uncomfortable. Still, if these were Nick's last days, he should know the truth.

"I never stopped loving you. See you on Friday."

40

Breaking the News

"You can't be serious."

Janice's mother sprinkled pepper into the food and stirred before turning to look at her daughter.

"You want to use my car to drive to Washington, DC? Are you crazy? For what?"

"I don't know. I just thought it was a good idea to see my dad face-to-face for who he is finally."

Janice's mother frowned and adjusted the flame on the stove.

"And out of nowhere, you want to drive to DC? Alone?"

"Why not? I'm old enough."

"Well, on top of it being a long trip, what am I supposed to do about a ride to work?"

"Why can't Michael take you? It's only one day."

"I don't know, Janice. Everything about this trip seems suspicious."

"Come on, mom. What do you think this trip is about?"

"Honestly?"

"Sure."

"It's either drugs or that damned Nick boy."

"You've got to be kidding me. I've been clean for months, and I haven't seen Nick in over a year."

"Uh-huh."

"I'm insulted, mom. Do my grades reflect a daughter spiraling out of control?"

"No. But then again, you've never been on front-street with what you've got planned."

"I would take a friend, but they've all gone away to college."

"Why not wait until Saturday so that I can drive with you?"

"How is that going to sit with Michael? You think he's going to be okay with you driving with me to see one of your ex-lovers?"

Janice's mother cracked a smile.

"He'd probably shit if I went to him and told him that."

"Or punch you in the face."

"Does your father know you're coming?"

"No. I figured I'd just show up."

"Horrible idea."

"Why?"

"You don't just do a pop-in on a man. You're bound to see something you don't want to see."

"I have no expectations other than having dinner with him."

"Still, I don't think you should just show up out of the blue."

"Look, mom. I've put off knowing who my father is for years. How can I move forward with this big chunk of my life missing? I can't, and it's unfair for you to expect me to be normal when I have no idea of where I come from."

"You come from me."

"I know you, but I don't know my father. There's a whole family I know nothing about."

"Look, baby. I can't stop you from seeing your dad. But I just want to be sure it's not some other issue."

"It's not, mom. I would tell you if it was."

"Okay. I'll let Michael know. Just be safe. Things haven't been good for either of us."

"I know. I'll be safe."

"Now go ahead and set the table for dinner."

Janice opened the cabinet and grabbed a stack of plates. As she walked past her mother, she kissed her on the cheek.

"Thanks for understanding."

"Yeah, yeah. Just be safe."

41

The Truth About the World

Friday finally came, and Janice jumped in her mother's car and started her journey. Although she downloaded the most popular navigation app for her phone, Janice still expected to get lost on her way to DC. She was pleasantly surprised when she arrived a full two hours before the time she'd agreed to meet Nick. Janice rode around the city, taking in all the things she'd only previously been able to see through public transportation.

Janice rode through Georgetown and marveled at how much she'd missed because of her limited budget. Next, Janice rode past the bookstore where she used to work. Although several things had changed about the city, nothing seemed to have changed about that place. She even saw her old manager standing outside smoking a cigarette. Janice thought about blowing her horn to get her attention, but she was too embarrassed about how she left, so she decided against it.

When she passed her old apartment building, cold shivers ran down her spine. The alley still had the same look of danger that almost took her life. Two new guys that she didn't know stood in the same spot her previous dealers had worked, trying their best to look like they belonged. It wasn't long before Janice started thinking of the drugs that pushed her to those street corners late at night. Turned off and afraid by how easily she could cop drugs once more, she left that part of town and made her way back to where she'd agreed to meet Nick.

When Janice pulled up in front of the train station, there was a large number of people entering and exiting the building. As she searched the crowd looking for Nick, she began to get nervous. Janice hadn't seen Nick in a long time and wasn't sure if she was ready to see him. Janice still felt a lot of anger at what he'd done and couldn't just ignore her feelings.

Soon another thought came into Janice's mind. Without thinking, she grabbed her purse, pulled out her driver's license and money, and put them into her socks.

Suddenly there was a knock on the passenger window of her car and Janice jumped. She looked over to see Nick was standing at her window – or at least a version of him was. The person standing at her window looked frail and barely able to stand. There was hardly any meat on his face, reminding Janice of one of those National Geographic photos of starving children she'd seen. His eyes seemed sunken into his skull like all of the life in him had been sucked out. There were sores at the corners of his mouth, and his lips were chapped and bleeding. Nick no longer had the long, beautiful hair that Janice had loved to touch. Now he had rough and bushy hair with bald patches in it that looked like someone had burned them there. Nick's teeth looked like he'd brushed with a combination of butter and coffee.

"You going to let me in or what?" Nick mouthed through the window.

Reluctantly, Janice hit the automatic unlock button.

"Wow. I thought you weren't going to come."

"I told you I would, so here I am."

Soon a disgusting smell filled the car that made Janice want to vomit. Nick had shit his pants.

"Nick, when was the last time you had a bath?"

"It hasn't been that long. The day before yesterday. Why?"

"You stink. I mean, you smell."

"Well, I've only..."

Suddenly the two doors opened behind Janice, and two more people hopped in.

"Hey! What the hell?" asked Janice as she turned around.

"Oh shit!" yelled another corpse that looked vaguely familiar. "Your girl came! Nick's got serious dick power."

Janice shot a look at Nick.

"What the fuck is this, Nick?"

"Just drive, and everything will be okay."

"I'm not going anywhere! Who the fuck are these dudes in my car?"

The man sitting directly behind Janice spoke up.

"Janice! I can't believe you don't remember me."

Janice turned to face the man. He looked just as disgusting as Nick, except he had a nappy beard with bumps sprinkled throughout it.

"I don't know you."

"It's me, babe! Danny from the club!"

Janice was shocked. Danny was no longer the chubby high-energy guy she'd met at the club. This guy was all bones and looked like a walking corpse.

"Danny?" she asked. "What happened to you?"

"Life, babe. Life."

Janice looked at the other guy sitting quietly on the other side of the backseat. He was equally unkempt and filthy, yet he didn't smile. He had an evil look on his face that frightened Janice.

"What do you guys want? I have to get back home soon," Janice angrily explained.

"Drive. We need to pick up something first," said Nick.

Janice shook her head and looked out the window for the nearest police officer. Nick wasn't sick with cancer. Nick was a drug addict.

"Look, you guys have to get out. I need to leave."

"Not yet. Not yet," replied Nick. "You got any money?"

It was at that moment that Janice noticed Nick's strange body movements. His eyes were shifty, and he was always moving from left to right. He licked his lips repeatedly, and he kept scratching – first his neck and then his arms.

"No, I don't have any money."

Suddenly the quiet guy spoke up from the back seat.

"She's lying, dude. How was she able to travel to DC without money?"

Nick grabbed Janice's purse.

"Hey! Nick, stop!"

Without hesitating, Nick slapped Janice, and she fell against the window.

"Where's the fucking money? Why are you hiding it? Give it up!"

Janice rubbed her cheek. She couldn't believe Nick hit her.

"I put it in the gas tank to come and pick you up!"

Once again, the guy from the backseat interfered.

"She's lying! How was she going to drive home? That bitch is lying!"

Janice turned and yelled her response to the guy in the back seat.

"My father lives here in DC! He was going to pay for my ride home!"

Nick looked up from rummaging through Janice's purse.

"Your dad lives here? In DC?"

"Yes, you jerk!"

"Does he have any money?"

"I don't know."

Nick tossed her purse onto the floor and pointed toward the road.

"Let's see what he has. Let's go."

"Where?"

Nick slapped Janice and pulled her hair.

"Stop playing fucking dumb! We're going to your dad's house!"

"But I don't..."

Nick slapped her again.

"If I have to tell you one more time, I'm going to seriously fuck you up!"

Danny punched the back of the driver's seat.

"You should kick her ass anyway. She's lying about the money. I know it!"

Janice was terrified. There was no telling what three drug addicts were capable of doing.

"I swear! I don't have any money!"

Nick looked at Janice and licked his lips.

"Let's go. Just drive the car."

Janice pulled out of the waiting area and onto the main road leading into the city. She had only driven one block when a black sedan pulled up in front of her car and blocked her from going further.

"What the fuck is this asshole's problem?" asked Nick.

Janice's eyes widened in surprise as her father climbed out of the car, put on some dark sunglasses, and walked up to the driver's side of the vehicle. With his keys, he tapped on the glass, and Janice rolled down the window.

"Yes?"

"Ma'am, I'm going to have to ask you to climb out of the vehicle."

Nick frowned in protest.

"Just like that? You don't want to see her license and registration? What the fuck kind of cop are you?"

Janice's father lowered his glasses and looked over at Nick.

"I'd suggest you keep your mouth closed if you boys hope to get out of this without visiting jail."

Janice's father opened the car door and grabbed Janice by her elbow.

"Is that your purse on the floor?"

"Yes."

The tall man reached into the car and grabbed the purse.

"Damn. You boys smell like shit," he mumbled as he grabbed Janice by her elbow again.

He calmly walked her to his car, opened the passenger door, and helped her sit inside. Janice's father climbed into the driver's seat and pulled away.

"How did you know where to find me?"

Alex held up his hand to silence Janice.

"Hold that thought one moment."

Alex pulled over to the side of the road and looked in his rearview mirror while Janice turned around to look back. Suddenly four black sedans surrounded the car.

"What's going on?" asked Janice.

"Something that should've happened to that group a long time ago," responded Alex.

Janice watched in horror as men dressed in dark suits poured from the vehicles and ran to her mother's car. After yanking on the locked doors, one of the men retrieved a crowbar from one of the sedans' trunks and smashed the windows.

"My mother's car!" yelled Janice. "What the hell?!"

"Relax. Your mom will receive payment."

The men yanked the drug addicts from the vehicle and slammed them roughly onto the ground. After handcuffing Nick and his drug addict friends, the men put the trio into the back of one of the vehicles.

"Are they going to jail? Are you going to hurt them?"

"No worries. They're going to rehab. They'll get the same help you got."

"What is it that you do?"

Alex ignored Janice's question and started the car again. As he pulled out onto the road, Janice continued to question him.

"How did you know I was coming to the city?"

"Your mom. She didn't trust the reason you gave her for coming to the city, and she thought you were coming to buy drugs. She reached out. I waited for you at the GW Parkway exit on 495."

Janice shook her head in disappointment.

"So typical. Mom never believes anything I say."

"Her guess wasn't far off."

"What do you mean?"

"I just pulled you from a car full of dope heads, right?"

"Nick told me he had cancer and needed a ride home. I came here to take him home because he begged me to come. I didn't know he would try to rob me."

"Well, it's over now."

The car drove on until they reached a nice neighborhood with expensive houses.

"So, this is where you stay?"

"Yeah."

"So that other apartment was for…"

"Work."

"And what kind of work is that again?"

"Let's have that conversation inside the house."

Finally, the car pulled in front of a large townhouse.

"Where's your wife?"

"Wife?"

"That's who you told me Tonya was, remember?"

"Tonya was my wife on that day. That's what I needed her to be until we got you out."

"So, she's not your wife?"

"No. Tonya's my colleague."

Alex climbed out of the car and walked to the front door. After unlocking the door, Alex stepped in, and Janice followed. Janice looked around the house and was surprised at what she saw. Although her father had the income to support a comfortable lifestyle, his home barely had furniture. Instead of a comfortable sofa and loveseat, three wooden chairs were sitting in the middle of the floor. The windows had heavy thick curtains that prevented any light from entering the house. There was a desk in the corner of the room with four computer monitors on it.

"Have a seat. Can I get you something to drink?" asked Alex after noticing the confused look on Janice's face.

Janice sat down in a chair and stared at her father.

"You can't be married."

"Why do you say that?"

"No woman on earth would live in such a cold, barren house."

"That's a bit harsh, isn't it?"

"Hey, I'm just speaking from a female's perspective."

Alex retrieved a soda from his refrigerator and gave it to Janice.

"So...where do we start?" he asked as he sat in the wooden chair across from her.

"I don't know. The beginning, maybe?"

Alex took a sip of his soda and belched.

"How about this. Let's start with what your mother told you about me and I'll either agree or set the record straight."

For a few minutes, Janice and her father Alex touched on light subjects such as the news, weather, and sports. But it wasn't long before Janice grew weary of small talk. She had so many questions for her father, and she didn't want to waste any more time. Finally, she asked a question.

"Why did you abandon my mother and me?"

The question didn't surprise Alex at all. Instead, it seemed to push his mind in many different directions at once; he took a deep breath, and then he exhaled; he squeezed his eyes shut and then opened them wide; he opened his mouth as if to speak, and nothing came out. After going through these strange rituals, Alex finally answered the question.

"Because I was a boy."

The response was so simple that it bothered Janice. She could feel her anger gathering like thunderbolts inside of a cloud, looking for a way to release the energy. She wanted to yell at her father, but instead, two soft words came out.

"I'm listening."

Alex stood and pulled on his shirt until most of the wrinkles were out. As he started talking, he walked into the kitchen to get another soda.

"Your mom and I were never supposed to hook up. Did your mom tell you that?"

"No."

"I slid her a note to pass to the girl sitting beside her in class. Like a dummy, I forgot to write the name of the other girl in the letter. Your mother thought I was trying to talk to her."

"Well, that was mighty smart of you."

"Yeah, I wasn't too bright back then. Anyway, we started talking, and we got close fast. Next thing you know, I was walking Shannon home from school every day, and we were taking lunches together in the cafeteria. One day I was walking her home, and it started raining. We sprinted down her street, both of us soaked from head to toe. When we made it to her front porch, we sat down on her porch swing and watched the thunderstorm. That's when I asked her to be my girlfriend."

"That was nice. Mom never told me about that."

"She probably wishes she could forget it. Anyway, we fell in love, and we started having sex."

"And then you left us."

Janice felt embarrassed for blurting out the obvious, but there was no way she was going to let her father romanticize what he did.

"It didn't happen like that. I was in love with your mother. Deeply in love. But teenagers are dumb as shit. Only teenagers with parents attached at the hip avoid tragedy growing up."

"Isn't that the truth."

"I had a couple of buddies of mine – John and Patrick. They introduced me to heavy metal and marijuana. Pretty soon, your mom was background noise in my life. I started to only visit when I wanted sex, and I stayed away when she complained about me not giving her time."

"And then you got her pregnant and left."

"I don't know if it was the weed or the immaturity. All I know is that when I found out your mother had cheated on me with one of the guys at our school, I flipped. I stopped talking to her altogether."

Janice looked surprised.

"What? She cheated on you?"

"Yep. I'm guessing your mother left out that part when she told you I left."

"Um, yeah. Mom left that out."

"Anyway, one day, Shannon caught me at school and told me she was pregnant. I didn't know what to think. We used to hear stories about girls that would trap innocent boys into taking responsibility for pregnancies. In my anger about her infidelity, I guess I conveniently forgot all the times we'd slept together without protection. I was confused, so I sought advice from my two brain-dead friends. They told me the name of the guy she cheated with – Michael."

"Michael? The man that she's married to now?"

"Yep. Everyone hated that guy's guts in school. He was a real prick. And when I found out he was sleeping with your mother, I flipped. The next day I left town."

"But why didn't you come back?"

"I thought about it, but every time I thought about your mother, I'd see Michael's face too. I began telling myself that the child was probably his. After a while, I started to believe it."

"And you left mom alone? How could you do that?"

Alex's face hardened as he looked at Janice.

"Which one of those boys in the car was Nick?"

"What?"

"Nick was your boyfriend, right? Which one was he?"

"I don't see how that's relevant."

"My guess is Nick was the one sitting in the passenger seat."

Janice didn't respond.

"Did he ever cheat on you?"

Janice looked away as she lied.

"No. The relationship didn't work out."

Alex cracked a smile and took another sip of his soda.

"Uh-huh. All I can say is, infidelity does something strange to your mind. It can make you hate someone. After I found out your mother cheated on me, I hated her. Pretty soon, it became one of those things where I just stopped giving a damn about anything associated with her."

"And leaving a woman and child didn't come into your thoughts?"

"Like it or not, cheating has consequences."

Janice shook her head in disgust.

"Oh my God," she whispered. "I can't believe this bullshit."

"What?" asked Alex.

"You mean to tell me that your male ego was so fragile that it would make you abandon a child?"

"As I said, your mother cheated. I'm sorry if that excuse isn't what you wanted to hear, but it's the truth."

Janice took another sip of her soda.

"So, where does that leave us now?"

Alex stood up and walked to the kitchen to place his can into the recycle bin.

"Look. I'm not here trying to erase what I did. In my mind, it's just the one dip in the road that sent me on a different path than your mother's. But I'm here and willing to build a friendship if you want one. I can't force my way into your life, and I'm not going to be one of those Leave It to Beaver dads. You and I have to find a way to push aside all the bad that has happened to make room for the good things to happen."

"How do I know you won't just abandon me whenever you see something you don't like?"

Alex returned to his seat.

"If hiding a murder and getting you help with your drug problem doesn't prove to you that I'm for real, then nothing will."

Janice finished drinking her soda and walked into the kitchen to place it into the recycle bin.

"There can't be secrets between us," she said as she returned to her chair.

Alex smiled.

"I wouldn't have it any other way."

"Cool. You can start by telling me about your job."

Alex started laughing.

"What's so funny?"

"I think you'd better call your mother to tell her you'll be home tomorrow. At this rate, we're going to be up all night talking."

"Do you have an air mattress?"

"Yep."

"I'll give mom a call now."

Alex passed Janice his telephone and smiled as his daughter dialed her mother.

9 781963 058017